String of Fate

Her Warriors

BIANCA D'ARC

This book is a work of fiction. The names, characters, places, and incidents are products of the writer's imagination or have been used fictitiously and are not to be construed as real. Any resemblance to persons, living or dead, actual events, locale or organizations is entirely coincidental.

No part of this book may be used or reproduced in any manner whatsoever without written permission, except in the case of brief quotations embodied in critical articles and reviews.

DEDICATION

Many, many thanks to my friend, Peggy McChesney, for taking the time to humor a crazed writer. Your help and support have been invaluable, as well as your friendship.

I think this time, I also have to thank the characters that just wouldn't let me end what had been planned as the *String of Fate TRILOGY* from the very beginning. Somehow, when I finished writing *Jacob's Ladder*, these three characters just wouldn't let me go. They wanted their story told and I didn't get the usual downtime I take between books. No, these characters just kept doing stuff in my head to the point where I feel almost as if the two books are one giant book in my heart.

Many thanks to Dad for putting up with canned/frozen dinners and eating out a lot, because I was hijacked by my fictional characters, and unable to interact with my family in the real world for a few weeks. The really sad part is, I'm not sure he actually noticed. LOL! Guess I'm not much of a cook anyway, so he was probably better off.

.

PROLOGUE

Geir Falkes, training master of those who would try to become Royal Guards for the queen of the *pantera noir*, was stuck. Not physically. There was little in this mortal realm that could slow down the man who was master of his own body and trained others to be the same. No, he was stuck about what he should do.

The Nyx—the queen he had chosen to serve—had been running all her life, until just recently. Last week, they had defeated her enemy in a fierce battle on a mountain ridge in North Carolina. This week, he was on another mountain, upstate New York, checking out a house he had just bought.

The house had a giant barn on the grounds. Few knew, that the so-called *barn* was really a state-of-the-art dojo and training center. It was the perfect place for him to teach new Royal Guards and work with those who were already qualified to protect the Nyx. Now that her most troublesome enemy had been dealt with, she was able to settle in one place. In fact, she had just bought the house near the top of this very same mountain, and all the land around it.

The place had been set up by the former king of tiger shifters, Frederick, and his wife, Candis. They had been in exile here in New York for decades, but their fortunes had recently changed. A new king had fought Frederick's brother—something Frederick could not do—and won. As it turned out, the new king was an old friend of Geir's, a former Royal Guard named Mitch.

Mitch had mated the tiger princess, Frederick and Caudis's only daughter, Gina. Shortly thereafter, the queen Geir served had mated a human warrior. Everybody was settling down, two by two. It felt like only Geir was still alone.

He finally had a home of his own, and no mate to share it with.

He had met a woman recently. She was a fascinating woman that made his tiger claw at his insides to be nearer to her. But she was already being courted by another of Geir's kind. Another tiger shifter. A soldier with anger issues, named Beau Champlain.

Beau was everything Geir was not. Younger. American. Handsome. Easy with his words. Geir had watched him interact with her—Jacki, was her name—and Geir had been envious for one of the few times in his life. There was no doubt Geir held higher rank among their people than Beau, but in this instance, Beau had it all over the Icelandic tiger who had spent all his life learning how to fight and teaching others to do the same.

Geir wasn't suave. He wasn't sophisticated. He wasn't very experienced with women outside of the encounters his inner tiger drove him to initiate. Geir lived the life of an ascetic for the most part. He had studied hard to become the master of fighting arts suitable to train the Royal Guard of the Nyx. And that was about all he had going for him, which didn't seem like a whole lot when he was interested in a woman as amazing as Jacki Kinkaid.

"The house is very large," Geir said to Tad Miller, one of the grown Miller children who had been raised on the property Geir had just bought. Tad was overseeing the transfer of the house and grounds for his parents, who were in Iceland.

"It had to be big with so many cubs in the family, plus all

the strays my folks took in." Tad smiled as they walked through the empty house. "This was a good home. Filled with love and learning. Discipline and care. I think that permeates the building still, and maybe one day you'll raise your own cubs here."

Geir wished that were so. But if he never got off his duff and found a way to speak to a woman—one special woman in particular—he would have a hard time fulfilling that dream.

"I'd have to find a mate first," Geir answered noncommittally. "If the Goddess so blesses me."

"No reason to think She won't." Tad smiled jovially. "I met Mandy young. In truth, we knew each other from the time we were both children, but we didn't recognize the fact that we were mates until we were older. When the time was right. And the Lady has already blessed us with our first cub. The first of many, we hope." Tad gazed into the distance for a moment, a smile on his face, before returning to the matter at hand. "As you can see, there's plenty of room in the main house. We've used this building as home, hospital, and boarding house for some of my dad's top students, among other things. You get the idea—it can serve many purposes. And there's lots of room to expand." It was clear the building had been well-used and much loved.

"Your parents don't ever intend to come back to the States?" Geir asked. He knew the elder Millers had moved back to Iceland and most of their grown children had become Royal Guards for the new tiger king. It was Mr. Miller who had trained all the Royal Guards for the tiger Clan—both before leaving Iceland and after he had chosen to go into exile with the true king.

It was more or less the same role Geir played for the Nyx, and this house and grounds would work nicely for his purposes. It had been built by tiger shifters and Geir himself was a tiger shifter, even though he had devoted his life to the smaller, more mysterious *pantera noir* Clan.

"They'll only come back for visits now, I think," Tad

answered. "Their true home is in Iceland, but they raised us kids as Americans, so the younger generation might want to come back occasionally. Which is why we'll sell you everything except the small cabin down at the lower end of the property, and my house, which is right next to it. Mandy and I are going to try splitting our time between here and Iceland for a while and figure out where we want to raise our cubs. Her parents went back to the old country too, but we were both raised here and it's a bigger adjustment for us."

"I can understand that," Geir agreed. "I was born in Iceland, but left at a young age. I've lived many places and though I could return to my birthplace now, it probably wouldn't feel like home."

"Well, this is a good place to settle," Tad observed. "It was good for us. We were happy here and I hope you will be too. Come on, let me show you the dojo."

They walked out of the main house and toward the very large barn that was set at some distance from the house. Geir liked the climate here. It was early autumn, and dusk was almost upon them. The air was cool and crisp at this elevation and Geir knew there would be plenty of snow come winter. He liked snow.

He had left Iceland barely a man, and wandered for a time before settling down with his aunt's adopted Clan. The *pantera noir* had made him welcome even though he was a golden tiger, a *tigre d'or*. With the tiger monarchy in chaos for the past few decades, Geir had had no alternative but to seek his fate elsewhere. He had found purpose for his life and all his training, in protecting one of the most vulnerable of the big cat monarchs.

Until the defeat of her greatest enemy just last week, Ria—the young Nyx—had lived her life constantly on the run. Never staying in one place too long, she needed round-the-clock protection by the most skilled of elite fighters. Royal Guards.

Geir had been training Ria's Guards for years now and he took pride in his work. His goal was to turn out warriors that would think outside the box and use a myriad of different skills and adaptations to keep their charge safe from harm. They had done their job well and Ria had been able to confront her enemy with her Guard at her side.

The battle had been ferocious. The mage who had been hunting Ria for years had an affinity for water and the creatures that lived in it. His strange tactics had worked for a while, but then Jacki Kinkaid had stepped in and done her magic. It was pure and good, and the tone of it sang through Geir's heart long after her spell had done its work.

Geir had admired Jacki's courage and marveled at her strength, even as he was staggered by her beauty. She had the kind of beauty that stunned. It shone from within, and the light in her soulful brown eyes was that of a creature who saw the good in all of creation. If she wasn't already, Geir had no doubt that Jacki would soon become a priestess of the Lady. Her soul was that pure. That good.

Geir had done his part to protect her during the aftermath of her spell, when her own power reserves were too low for her to even move. He had hidden her in a circle of bushes and done his best to protect her. The other tiger shifter—Beau—had done his part too, climbing a tree above her and acting as a sniper, keeping the enemy well away from her hiding place.

But then Beau had been shot and he had fallen hard, right out of the tree. Geir had dragged the other man into the hiding spot and tried to help him. And then Jacki had turned the tables and trapped Geir inside a dome of protection she created with the very last of her power.

Geir had been torn from the very beginning of the battle. His heart wanted him to stay at Jacki's side and keep her from all harm, but his duty lay with the Nyx. It was his place to protect the queen and fight alongside those he had trained—to the last man, if necessary.

During the initial strategy session, Geir and Beau had been placed with Jacki and her brother, Tom. Jacki and Tom were both highly-magial selkies—seal shifters—and their mission was to look after the waterways on the mountain. But they needed backup to help watch their backs while they watched over the waterways. Tom had taken the lake and had been quickly overrun.

Geir had been with Tom and was eventually able to push back the attack enough to get Tom clear. He was badly injured and Geir had brought him to where Jacki was hiding. And then she had sealed all four of them—the two wounded, herself and Geir—inside a magical circle from which he could not escape.

He still didn't really understand why she had done it. She had begged his forgiveness before she cast the spell that left her unconscious. That told him she knew he would have had to leave her side to fight with the Royal Guard elsewhere, but why she had kept him from his duty remained a mystery.

Had she meant to protect him? Or had she simply run out of time to let him out of the circle before she cast it? Was he included in her spell by design—which might mean she cared for him—or was it simply an accident?

Either way, Geir had spent the rest of the battle inside an almost impenetrable dome, tending three wounded and looking for a way to get out so he could rejoin his comrades. It wasn't until the battle was well and truly over that someone discovered them, and helped bring down the ring of protection from the outside.

By then, Geir was at his last shred of patience and frustration. He had simply picked Jacki up in his arms and carried her down the mountain. He hadn't known what to say to the queen he had sworn to protect. He hadn't been there for her, but she didn't seem to mind. Those he had trained in her Guard had taken casualties, but to his surprise, none of them looked at him with disdain either. Somehow the fact that he had been unable to fight with them didn't seem to matter to them.

But it mattered to Geir.

How could Jacki have done that to him? And had it been on purpose? Her motivation somehow mattered more than the act itself. She had recovered from the ordeal, but he hadn't had much chance to talk with her. She had spent almost all her time at Beau's side, caring for him as he healed, and Geir had left North Carolina before he'd had a chance to get a moment alone with her.

But even if he had managed to corner her away from everyone else, what would he have said? Geir wasn't the most eloquent of men. Far from it. English wasn't even his first language and Jacki sure as hell didn't know Icelandic. How was he to express himself when he wasn't even sure what he wanted to ask or how he could possibly do it in a way that didn't expose him to either ridicule or pity if she rejected him?

What it boiled down to was that Master Geir—badass sensei of the elite *pantera noir* Royal Guard—was scared. Of a woman. Who could possibly wound him more deeply than any other creature on earth.

CHAPTER ONE

Jacki Kinkaid was mostly recovered from the huge expenditure of energy she had made during the battle. She was better physically, but emotionally, she was all at sea. She had stayed in North Carolina, wanting to help nurse the injured, but they hadn't really needed her. The fox Pack that ruled the territory had an abundance of highly trained medical personnel in its ranks, and didn't really need her amateurish attempts at nursing.

So she had spent a lot of time at Beau Champlain's bedside. He had been unconscious a lot of the time, but yesterday he had taken a turn for the better. He was awake and as frisky as any tiger shifter left too long idle. He wanted to go, go, go, but the doctors wouldn't let him, and they had appealed to Jacki to sit on him if she had to, to make him stay in bed.

Why that simple phrase had brought such a blush to her cheeks, she didn't know, but when one of the well-meaning doctors said the same thing in front of Beau, the frisky tiger shifter had winked at her. That little, knowing wink had set her cheeks aflame and she had fled quickly, seeking a moment alone to calm herself.

Jacki was a selkie by birth—a seal shifter about whom many legends existed from the old country of Ireland. Not much of the old stories were factually accurate. For example, she didn't have a seal skin she put on like a coat and had to hide when she took human form on land. She was a shifter like any other. Her two forms simply came when she called them. No icky skin suits involved.

But selkies were a little different than other shifters too. For one thing, they were way more magical than most. And Jacki herself was discovering a deeper well of magic inside herself than she had previously realized. She had trained to use her magic most of her life, but just recently her personal power had ramped up a notch...or three. She wasn't sure why or how, but she definitely felt a need to learn more about why she was suddenly so much more powerful magically than she had ever been.

Selkies of the Irish myths were purported to be beautiful. Jacki had never felt it. Sure, she knew her brother and her kin were above-average handsome, but they were her family. She would love them regardless of what they looked like. Jacki herself perpetually fought against the fat her seal form wanted to line every part of her body with. Sure, it would keep her warm in the ocean, but on dry land, Jacki sometimes felt more like a whale than a seal. At least compared to the svelte ground-based female lion shifters in her Clan.

There were more than a few selkies in the Kinkaid Clan too, of course, but most of the Clan was made up of lions. They were tall and lithe, the women were fit and some were skinny in a way Jacki would never be. After all, she was a seal when she shifted. Not a sleek jungle cat.

And she thought she resembled her seal in human form too. In a word—fat. Maybe she didn't have Jabba-the-Hut style body rolls, but she was definitely a lot curvier than her lion shifter cousins. She had hips. Big hips. And though she was as strong and as flexible—if not more so—as her lion shifter cousins, she was shorter and plumper than any of the lion girls she had grown up with.

It had made Jacki shy. And though, like most shifters, she'd had her share of sexual experiences over the years, she had never formed any long-term relationships with men. The longest her relationships lasted were a few weeks. Usually less. It was kind of depressing and it didn't give her a whole lot of experience dealing with attractive men on a long-term romantic basis.

When she fled Beau's knowing smirk, she headed for her comfort place—the water. Higher up on the mountain ridge, the small lake and stream running near the stone circle sacred to the Goddess beckoned. Jacki intended to seek the lake, but instead found herself at the stream in the very place she had fought in the last battle.

She didn't know where the strength had come from to do what she had done all those days ago. Jacki hadn't even known she *could* do something like that before it had happened. She was still a little shocked by it. But her beloved Aunt Sophia was a seer. She had told Jacki where to go and hinted at what to do. Aunt Sophia's words had given her the guts to try.

When Jacki's cell phone rang, she almost laughed. That ring tone was the one she had assigned to her aunt. Sure enough, as Jacki answered the phone, her aunt's voice came to her over the connection.

"Are you at the stone circle?"

No hello. That meant her aunt was on the move. Impatient. It was a quirk of hers when she was in the grips of a vision, or shortly thereafter. Jacki knew enough not to argue or delay. Her aunt's visions were powerful and they demanded a lot of the woman. Jacki wouldn't complicate matters by fooling around at a time like this.

"Not quite," she replied just as abruptly. "I'm at the stream, just below the circle."

"Go to the circle. Go now," Sophia urged.

"All right." Jacki was moving quickly through the woods as she spoke. She broke through the last of the sheltering trees and into the small stone circle, hidden among them.

"Is she there?" Sophia's voice was hushed, almost reverent.

Jacki looked into the circle and it was glowing with an unearthly light. In the center of the circle, by the stone altar, was a being. The small creature was human-shaped, but this was no human. Not by a long shot. Jacki blinked and tried to focus her eyes on the person in the center of the circle.

"Someone's there. It's glowing," she told her aunt in a whisper.

"Good." Sophia sounded relieved. "I'll hang up now. Go to her. She'll tell you what comes next. Good luck, little one. I've always had faith in you. It's time you found your own faith."

And with those characteristically cryptic words, her aunt hung up. Jacki returned the phone to her pocket and squared her shoulders. Her aunt wouldn't have led her into anything bad. Quite the opposite. If Aunt Sophia wanted her to be here to meet this person, it must be a good thing. An important thing.

The question was…did Jacki have the guts to meet her destiny?

Well, there was no time like the present to find out. Jacki braced herself and walked into the stone circle.

"Hello, child." The voice came from the glowing being at the center of the circle. It was a voice filled with music and clear tones that touched something deep inside Jacki. "Be welcome here."

The closer she stepped, the more she was able to see the being. It was a woman. A petite woman with a fey grace. Jacki had seen this woman before. Only once, but she had made an impression.

"High Priestess?" Jacki was confused and it sounded in her tone.

"Call me Bettina, child. For you are soon to be one of us. One of the Lady's priestesses." Bettina's smile lit the circle with its warmth.

"You're kidding." It wasn't an elegant answer, but the High Priestess had just floored Jacki.

Bettina's musical laugh floated through the circle, echoing

off the standing stones with a chiming sound.

"Nope. Not kidding." Her expression sobered a bit. "What you did here during the last battle proved your worth and your dedication to the Goddess. You skipped all the normal training and went straight for the big banana. You called on the Lady's power when it was most needed and She favored you. You are already Her servant whether you realize it or not. She has chosen you. All that remains is for you to be consecrated—if you agree."

"Big banana?" Jacki was dumbfounded by what Bettina had said, but her mind was stuck on hearing such casual words from such an exalted being. Bettina wasn't human. At least not completely. She hid it well, but Jacki had always suspected the small woman of immense power was at least part fey.

Bettina laughed again, her eyes crinkling a little at the corners—the only sign of any age at all on her beautiful face. Yet, she was older than Jacki's own mother. Bettina had been the High Priestess of the Lady for as long as anyone could remember. Which, for shifters with exceptionally long life spans, was a very long time indeed.

"You expected me to be more formal with a lot of thees and thous in my sentences?" Bettina walked closer and the glow diminished even more until she was just a very pretty woman, no magical aura around her at all.

And she was short. A lot shorter than Jacki. Which seemed incongruous since the woman had such immense power.

"Sorry?" Jacki wasn't sure how to respond.

"It's okay, Jacqueline. I suspect we'll get to know each other much better before all is said and done." Bettina began walking slowly and Jacki naturally fell into step beside her.

"Call me Jacki. And why do you think that?"

"Well, for one thing, you accomplished a task here a few days ago that would have been impossible for almost anybody else. It makes me think that perhaps I've finally found my successor."

"What?" Jacki was hearing things, surely.

Bettina turned to look at her and they both stopped walking. "Think about it. The High Priestess has to be the most magical of all the Lady's priestesses. You're a selkie. You're used to being more magical than most shifters. And you—either knowingly or unknowingly—called on the Lady's power in that last battle and She answered you in terms no other priestess alive today could have handled. Yet you took all that power in stride. I think you were born to serve Her and it only took that battle to bring out your true talents."

"But I'm not even a priestess. I've never trained—"

Bettina cut her off with a gentle raised hand. "Sometimes it happens that way. In fact, it happened that way to me. I was just a regular girl doing regular things when a crisis hit and I asked for help from the Goddess. She chose to answer my plea. That's what happened to you too, Jacki. I think it's clear that you're to be my successor, if I should fall in the coming battle."

"Then you feel it too?" Jacki whispered, afraid to give voice to her fears. "That the worst hasn't happened yet?"

Bettina nodded with a solemn expression. "As far as I'm concerned, more and increasing conflict is a given. We have little time left to prepare and that includes securing a succession, in case it's needed. I think it's pretty clear, you are the one I've been waiting for." Bettina began walking again and Jacki followed at her side. "I thought it was Allie at first, but she was meant for the Lords. She is a good priestess and will lead all the North American *were* as their spiritual guide, but she is not destined to take my place as High Priestess. She hasn't got quite enough magical power. But you, my friend, are another animal altogether."

They walked in silence for a moment until they came to the stream, where the battle had taken place. Bettina stopped in the exact spot where Jacki had cast the counter-spell that had turned the tide of the battle for the lake and stream.

"You did good work here, child. The waters still hum with purity, and a trace of the Lady's magic." Bettina bent to run her fingers through the clear mountain stream. "The question remains, did you know what you were doing when you called on the Lady's mercy?"

Jacki knew there was no other path but honesty here. "No, milady." Jacki looked down at her feet, feeling a bit foolish. "I've been wondering where all that magic came from, but I didn't even dare consider the Lady might have answered my prayer Herself."

Bettina smiled and stood. "Don't worry. I didn't realize it, when it happened to me, either. The more I hear from you, the more I think She has a bigger plan for you. So let's talk." She started walking again, heading back toward the stone circle at a leisurely pace. "I've been making my home with the Lords, but I think I'm due a vacation, and I hear the Nyx is setting up shop in the mountains of New York. Lovely area this time of year," she said, almost conversationally. "If you were to accept Ria's invitation and your suitor's urging to go up there yourself, I think we could spend a little time honing your skills. And I could teach you the secret handshake."

"Secret handshake?" Bettina's figures of speech would take some getting used to. As Jacki thought that, she realized she had already made her decision. "Well, okay. I guess I'm New York bound. But how did you know Beau had been pestering me to go there?"

Bettina just smiled in that mysterious way of hers.

CHAPTER TWO

Beau Champlain didn't like being bedridden. For a shifter who normally healed faster than any human could imagine, it was a rare thing to have an injury that kept him immobile for more than a few hours. His inner tiger was clawing at his insides to get out and *run*.

But the doctors had strictly forbidden it.

Normally, a shift would help heal him, but in this particular instance, the wound had been caused by something poisoned with silver. A silver tipped, exploding bullet, packed with silver dust. An ugly piece of work designed to kill vampires outright and maim shifters for life—if they lived through it.

No wonder Beau had felt like shit for days after the battle. He had been unconscious mostly, but he remembered each time he woke, she was there. His angel in a seal skin coat. Only she wasn't wearing her fur when she mopped his brow and said little prayers to the Lady under her breath that she probably thought he was too messed up to hear.

Jacki Kinkaid had tended him while he'd been down and out, and it touched him more than he could say. There was no doubt in his mind that he wanted her for his own, but she was a selkie—a totally different species. She was curvy and luscious, and he practically salivated every time he got a look at her. He had no idea if they were even compatible, and he hadn't been lucid enough to discover if she really was his mate, or if he was just dreaming.

He thought she might be though. All the signs were there. He couldn't stop thinking about her. He felt a deep-seated need to kiss her…and more. He wanted to be with her all the time. It was like an obsession of the nicest, most pleasurable kind, which promised good things if, indeed, she turned out to be his mate in truth.

The only real way to know for sure was to get close to her. To kiss her, and see if she brought out his beast in human form. If she could make him purr while he was human, well, that would be undeniable confirmation that she was meant to be his. Beau couldn't wait to get back on his feet and kiss her. But he had to catch her first.

Jacki had proved quite elusive since he'd woken up, lucid for the first time in days. And then the Nyx and her new mate had left North Carolina to set up their new place in New York. The Nyx had come personally to invite Beau to join them there while he convalesced. He hadn't given her an answer. He couldn't. He technically still worked for the Kinkaids and had to clear his movements with them. The last assignment he'd been given was to keep Jacki safe. She was a full-blooded Kinkaid, after all. And Beau was loyal to the Clan and its leader, Sam Kinkaid, king of all lion shifters and self-made Texas billionaire.

As long as Jacki was here in North Carolina, Beau would stay here too—even if he was no good for keeping her safe at the moment. In fact, it was more the other way around. She had nursed him through a hellacious poisoned bullet wound. The roles had reversed. She had protected him after he fell from his sniper's nest in the battle, and she had been looking after him ever since.

Well, no more. He had urged her to accept the Nyx's invitation to go to New York. That way, he could go with her, continuing to follow his last order to keep her safe while she was away from her Clan.

Jacki's brother, Tom, was wounded too, and was in even worse shape than Beau. She had spent her time split between them and now that Beau was on the mend, she seemed to be spending more and more time with her brother—which was only right, but it stuck in Beau's craw. He wanted her attention on him.

As much as he liked Tom, Beau didn't want to share Jacki with anyone. Not yet. Not until he'd figured out whether or not she was really his mate. It was driving his tiger crazy, being so near her and yet so far. The tiger didn't understand inaction. It paced around inside Beau's skull, wanting to do something, roaring at his human half to get a move on already.

So when Jacki came back from a walk in the woods and brought the fresh scent of the outdoors right to his bedside, he felt like he'd won the lottery. She sat in the chair beside him and met his gaze with a bubbling sort of happiness, mixed with a new serenity that she hadn't had before.

He had been studying her for days and she'd seemed confused at times. Restless and edgy. Whatever had just happened, had calmed her. It had brought her a modicum of peace. And for that, Beau was glad.

"Where've you been?" he asked in a gentle voice he reserved only for her.

"I took a walk up to the stone circle."

"Alone?" Beau didn't like that. He wanted her protected at all times.

But she just smiled. "It's safe now. And I wasn't alone."

Jealousy hit him like a freight train, and for a moment, Beau couldn't breathe.

"The most extraordinary thing happened," she went on, seemingly oblivious to his upset. "The High Priestess was there." Beau's anger cooled a bit, replaced by curiosity. He was a cat, after all. "And she said the most amazing things." Jacki trailed off, her gaze going hazy as if in memory. It took her a moment, but she came back to him and smiled once more. "I'm going with you to New York. Bettina's going there too, and she's going to train me. I'm going to be a priestess."

Beau was dumbfounded, and he said the first thing that popped into his head. "I thought you already were." Her gaze narrowed in confusion, so he tried to clarify. "After what I saw you do to those creatures and all the magic you were able to pull from the water and earth and living things… I felt that, Jacki, and I've only ever felt something like that happen in the presence of a priestess."

"Well, I'm not. Not officially. Not yet." She refocused her gaze and met his. She looked…resolute, he thought. "But I will be."

A couple of days later, Beau was in much better shape. He was almost fully healed and working on getting back to his former state of battle-readiness. He had accompanied Jacki and Tom Kinkaid, along with a few more of the wounded, and those who had been invited to join the *pantera noir* queen and her new mate in their new stronghold.

The first stop on their agenda, once they'd reached the mountain, was to go up to the main house near the pinnacle of the mountain. They were to be formally received by the Nyx and her mate in their new territory. From there, all the newcomers would be assigned to places that best suited their condition, training and inclination.

The mountain was a vast place, with multiple residences and defensive positions. No matter where they tried to put him, Beau was ready to argue that his only proper place was at Jacki's side. He would get Sam Kinkaid involved, if he had to.

But Beau shouldn't have worried. The royal reception was way less formal than he was expecting. Ria and Jake—the Nyx and her human mate—were friendly, informal people. They welcomed Jacki with a hug and Beau with smiles, a backpounding handshake from Jake and a quiet inquiry about his injury from Ria. They made him feel welcome, appreciated and…almost like part of the family. Which was odd, to say the least.

Most shifter groups were based around a common species. Wolves had Packs. Lions had Prides. Other kinds of shifters had Clans or Tribes, or whatever worked best for their particular species.

Beau had always been a loner, going his own way and making a place for himself in various places. The most recent place he'd found was among the Kinkaid Clan. He felt good there. Most of the Kinkaids were big cats too. Lions, in fact. They understood that a big cat needed to run from time to time, and roar when the mood struck. They hadn't minded Beau's unusually volatile temper. In fact, they'd pummeled him and been pummeled in return, with good nature, when their cats rode them too hard.

A bit to Beau's surprise, Jake told him Master Geir had offered rooms at his place for Tom and Jacki Kinkaid and Beau, as their liegeman, to stay and convalesce. Beau had liked the other tiger shifter and thought they had worked pretty well together during the last battle—until Beau had gotten shot. He didn't remember much after that, but he did recall the rather humiliating necessity of Geir hauling him around like a sack of potatoes. He owed Geir big time for saving his ass. And wasn't that going to be humbling, having to thank the guy? But it had to be done. It was a matter of honor.

Beau might try to seem casual in his attitudes towards most things, but he was big on loyalty and honor. That was at the base of why he'd chosen to remain a lone tiger rather than pledge himself to the usurper ruler of his species who had been recently overthrown. Beau could have gone back to the *tigre d'or*, now that there was a new king and the usurper and his cronies had been dealt with, and maybe he still would. But for the moment, Beau was content to stay allied with the Kinkaids.

Especially now that he thought he might have a shot at finding a mate among them. Mating was not to be trifled with. If Jacki was meant to be his—and he hers—he would move heaven and earth, and forsake all other allegiances, to be with her. Mating was *that* important.

Ria and Jake had someone drive the trio down to Geir's place, which was a little farther down the mountain. Beau wondered what kind of place it was. He had heard rumors about this very special mountain and its facilities, but he was quickly learning that the rumors were pale reflections of the reality.

The first sight he had of Master Geir's new house was impressive. It was built in old farmhouse style and it was pretty darn huge. Antique-looking, it fit into the surroundings beautifully. When the dirt road widened, Beau saw that the house was only a small part of a compound that consisted of several outbuildings, including a huge barn that didn't really look like it contained livestock.

First of all, most prey animals like horses, cows, sheep and the like, wouldn't be very comfortable around a tiger shifter like Master Geir or his students. Secondly, what would he do with livestock? Geir didn't strike Beau as a gentleman farmer. In fact, he was anything but. Geir was called *Master* because he had earned the right to train all the *pantera noir* Royal Guards, and approve those that eventually took their place protecting the Nyx.

It was a hell of a responsibility. Only the most talented of fighters earned such an honor. Geir had to be an expert in many different disciplines in order to give his pupils the widest possible training. Beau looked forward to getting back in shape, and he hoped they were here long enough for him to put Geir through his paces—or, more likely, the other way around. It would be good to spar with one of his own species again. It had been a long time. Perhaps too long…

Geir saw the van coming down from the big house. He had been living here only a few days, but the place already felt like home. It helped that the remaining Millers—Tad and his mate, Mandy—had made him feel so welcome in their former family home. Tad and Mandy lived down at the edge of the vast property and Tad had been helping Geir the past few days, cleaning up and getting ready for more people to inhabit the place.

And here came the first few newcomers. Geir could hardly suppress his tiger's desire to pace. She would be here soon. As would the other tiger. Geir wasn't sure how he felt about Beau's presence. He knew the other tiger had the potential to be a rival for Jacki's attention, but while one part of him resented the idea, the tiger inside him looked forward to being around another of his kind again.

He had been training *pantera noir* for many years now. He liked the queen, and the various family lines that bred black panthers of different species—mostly leopard and puma. But there was something about being near other tigers. This house, for example, had been built by tigers and made comfortable specifically for tigers. The very wood was permeated with tiger scent and it made Geir feel welcome on an unconscious level.

Geir walked out the front door, wiping his hands on a rag as he went. He wanted to greet the new arrivals, but he didn't really have time to clean up. He'd been working on a few repairs around the house and was wearing serviceable work clothes—jeans and a T-shirt. Not his best, but it would be okay, he hoped. He wasn't sure what he should do to greet Jacki Kinkaid, but suspected that if he tried to dress up—or do anything too far out of the ordinary for him—he would only end up looking like a fool.

The van pulled up by the front door and Geir helped Jacki hop down from the front seat. He must have paused a little too long, feeling shaken by her presence. She smelled so damn good, it scrambled his senses for a moment. Luckily, she came to his rescue.

"It's good to see you again, Master Geir." Jacki's soft voice floated up to him and shook him out of his frozen state. He let go of her hand and stepped aside so she could move away from the van. "Thank you for putting us up while my brother and Beau get back on their feet."

"I'm happy to have you here," Geir said, going with her to open the back doors and help her brother get out of the van.

He looked worse than Geir had expected. Weak as a kitten and pale, as if he was very ill. Geir's brow furrowed. He had seen something like it before, and knew the other man's continued weakness wasn't a good sign.

Beau came around from the other side of the van and stood next to Geir as the two selkie siblings headed toward the front door. Geir sensed the other tiger's presence, but it was a welcome feeling, not the combative response he'd half-expected from his inner beast. As the brother and sister moved slowly into the house, Geir stopped Beau with a restraining hand on his arm.

"How long has he been like this?" Geir asked urgently.

"Since the battle. He hasn't rallied and frankly, I'm worried, but his sister is still in denial."

"The heart sees what it wants to see," Geir reflected, then turned to face Beau. "It's good to have you here, brother. Whatever else may happen, I am glad of your presence. I've been too long away from other tigers."

Beau seemed surprised, but Geir didn't give him a chance to respond. His guests were waiting for him to direct them and the selkie male would need to find his rest sooner rather than later, if Geir was any judge. He vowed to do all he could to help Tom. Geir would consult with every last healer he knew, including the snowcat elders in Tibet, if it would help the other man.

For Tom was Jacki's brother, and Geir didn't want to see her grieve for her brother. If there was anything Geir could do, he would do it. Sadly, he feared it wouldn't be enough to save Jacki's brother.

Geir entered the front hall, glad to see that he hadn't kept Jacki and Tom waiting too long. They were admiring the front foyer which, while not exactly grand in the traditional sense, was large, welcoming and homey. Geir liked the feel of the place and he could tell from their expressions that the selkie siblings did too.

"This place is beautiful," Jacki said, confirming Geir's hunch.

"It's big," Geir agreed. "A tiger couple built it and lived here, raising their many cubs, which makes it ideal for our purposes at the moment. There are several bedrooms on the first floor. Let me show you the options." Geir led the way down the hall, moving slowly in consideration of Tom's injuries.

"I've moved in to the room at the far end of the hall for the time being," Geir told them as they walked along. "The upstairs still needs a little work. The house was in very good repair, but I decided to do a little upgrading while everything was empty and easy to work around."

They stopped at the first door and Geir reached around to open it. "This is typical of the rooms on this floor, and most have their own attached bath." He went inside and opened the inner door that led to the gleaming white bathroom, so they could see it.

"We've got a winner," Tom said in a voice filled with relief. "If nobody minds, I'll just park myself here for now. You guys go on ahead. I'll just rest for a bit."

Jacki was at Tom's side, helping him to the freshly made bed. She drew back the covers as her brother kicked off his shoes and sat wearily on the side of the bed. She helped him settle, and tucked him in with obvious love and care. Geir felt a pang in the region of his heart even as his spine tingled with alarm. Something was very wrong with Tom. Geir very much feared they were going to lose him.

Geir didn't care to think what that would do to Jacki. It would be awful for her. Geir didn't want to see her in any kind of pain—especially not the pain of losing a brother. Geir had been there, done that, and wouldn't wish that on anyone. Especially not a woman as special as Jacki Kinkaid.

Tom insisted he would be fine and that he just wanted to rest for a bit. Eventually, Jacki was convinced to go find her own room. She joined Geir and Beau in the hallway. There was no question but that she would take the room right next to her brother's. It also just happened to be the room next to Geir's.

Beau settled on the room across the hall from Jacki's and dropped his gear before rejoining them. Jacki had asked to see where the kitchen was. She also wanted a tour of the rest of the house. Beau joined them.

Geir enjoyed showing his guests around—particularly Jacki, of course—but he found rather surprisingly, that he enjoyed Beau's observations about each new defensive position and chamber in the building. The house had been built with defense in mind and Geir was pleased that Beau caught on to that fact rather easily. It wouldn't be obvious to most, but Beau seemed to see beyond the walls and into the function of the design.

After the tour, Jacki and Beau each headed to their rooms to unpack and get comfortable. Eventually, they all ended up back in the kitchen and Geir realized it was almost lunch time. Jacki offered to make tea while Geir got to work on the meal he had planned once he'd heard he was going to have guests. It was kind of sad how much thought he had put into this meal and all the other preparations he'd made for their arrival. Geir didn't like being solitary, though that had been his path more often than not. With Jacki here, he had a chance to discover if maybe—just maybe—he would no longer have to walk his path alone.

If she turned out to be his mate, as he very much suspected she was, he would count himself the luckiest bastard to ever roam the earth. But he had to get close enough to her first, to find out if what he suspected was true. He had to kiss her, but it wasn't in Geir's nature to accost a lady on short acquaintance. He would have to find a way to work up to it slowly, in the natural course of things.

Somehow.

"There's a small farm on the other side of the valley that supplies meat for us. They were given startup capital by the tigers who lived here before and have a top notch organic operation. The steaks are some of the best I've ever eaten," Geir promised as he grilled the aforementioned steaks on the state of the art kitchen grill.

The big kitchen gleamed with stainless steel, professional-quality equipment. Everything was built on the large side, and built to last. Geir liked it and was pleased to see that his guests appreciated it too.

"Anything to drink other than tea?" Beau asked.

"In the fridge," Geir answered, still working at the grill. "Help yourself."

Beau reached into the gleaming metal refrigerator and took out a bottle of beer, automatically getting one for Geir, which was nice of him. Beau popped the tops off and handed the cold bottle to Geir as he came over to admire the grill and the bounty upon it.

"This is quite a place," Beau observed. "Thanks for putting us up."

"You are more than welcome here," Geir said, being sure to include Jacki by meeting her gaze briefly. "It's a big place for a bachelor, though I suspect it'll fill up fast once the rest of the Nyx's people get here. They intend this compound to function as a garrison and first line of defense, which is similar to how the tigers used it."

"How many can you fit in the house?" Jacki asked, looking around again as if to try to calculate how many people would fit into the rooms he had showed her.

"This was home to a rather large family of tiger shifters, but you might've noticed some of the outbuildings as you drove up. A couple of those structures can function as barracks and there are cabins all around the property, and all around the mountain, in fact. The idea would be to have everyone train here in the dojo—the big barn you probably saw as you drove up—and live in various locations around the perimeter of the mountain, similar to the way the tigers ran it. We're moving a few things around, of course," Geir added. "We need to make this place our own and not rely completely on all the work done by the *tigre d'or*. It'll be good for the Nyx's Clan to have permanent homes near her, for those that choose to move here."

"Clan Kinkaid is a little different from most others since we've got two major groups of shifters under our banner, though there are way more lions than there are selkies," Jacki observed. "Still, the *pantera noir* is something else altogether, since black cats can come from a variety of species."

"And the Nyx has been on the run almost all her life," Beau put in. "No roots. It's hard to run a Clan when you don't have a base of operations anywhere."

Geir was pleased they both seemed to realize the challenges Ria would face in uniting her scattered people.

"That's all going to change now," Geir said, as if making a promise to himself. "She's going to make her stand here and her Royal Guard will follow her anywhere. They will form the nucleus of the Clan, as they have for many years."

"How did you come to be the Master of the *pantera noir* Royal Guard?" Jacki asked. Geir's tiger strutted around inside his brain, pleased that its potential mate was curious about his background.

"I was born in Iceland, as you can probably tell from the accent I have never quite managed to lose." Geir paused to smile. His story wasn't exactly a cheery one, and he wasn't sure he'd be able to tell all of it. It wasn't really a secret—just something he preferred not to discuss most of the time. But if he was going to tell anyone, it would be Jacki. And he realized he didn't really mind Beau hearing it either. Beau was a brother, of sorts. A lone tiger who had chosen a solitary path. If anyone would understand Geir's choices, Beau probably would.

"A lot of tigers live there," Beau added, nodding. "Not my people, but some of our relatives, I think. Did you leave when King Frederick went into exile?"

"Yes," Geir confirmed. "Right around that time."

CHAPTER THREE

Geir couldn't quite bring himself to explain exactly why he had left Iceland. He let them think it was because of the king's exile—and it was connected in a way—but Geir's true reason for leaving was much more personal and too painful to poke at right now. It was enough he was telling them anything about that time. He rarely spoke of it. This new openness would take some getting used to.

Baby steps. That's what he needed here. Small disclosures over time, so the pain wouldn't be so raw. It was his chosen strategy, and he was going to stick to it for now.

"I was young, though," Geir continued. "I went to my aunt, who had married into the *pantera noir*. The former Master saw to my training and sent me abroad when I needed to learn certain skills he could not teach me. Eventually, I ended up in the snowcat enclave in Tibet. That's where I first heard about Jake, the Nyx's new mate. He's something of a legend there. He may be only human, but he earned the respect of the snowcat elders, which is a rare feat. Jake is a force to be reckoned with, no doubt about it. He will be good for Ria. For too long has she been alone with her burden. It's good that they found each other."

Now, how had he gotten onto that subject? Mating wasn't something Geir ever really talked about, but he guessed maybe his inner tiger was pushing the thought into his brain. The cat wanted to find out if Jacki was the woman for them. It thought she was already, but it needed confirmation. And his human side definitely needed that confirmation before he could commit his emotions any further.

"They're a really good couple," Jacki agreed with a wistful sort of look on her face that Geir understood all too well.

"So how did you get from Tibet back to the Nyx? I've heard that few who train with the snowcats find their way back home. Although…I guess Iceland is your home," Beau observed, a question in his tone.

"No, my home is with the Nyx now. I'm sworn to her service and more than that, I fit in here. I know I'm needed. If the day ever comes when I'm not, or I fail to serve her to the best of my ability, I'll leave. For now though, I choose to stay with her."

Whoa. He hadn't meant to get quite so serious. He needed to lighten the mood, but Geir wasn't much good at conversation. His social skills were already stretched and they had only just arrived. He definitely had an uphill battle on his hands here, but he wasn't a quitter. Geir smiled as he finished off the steaks and began putting them on plates.

"Besides…" he tried for a joke, "…have you seen the tiger stronghold in Iceland? It's really cold there on the glacier. I may have a fur coat, but I don't like to freeze all the time." They smiled as they helped themselves to the side dishes they had all helped prepare. He put the sizzling steaks on the table. "Should we call Tom or bring him something later?" he asked, thinking of the missing man from their group.

"He's sleeping," Jacki said, a worried look on her face. "I peeked in on my way here. I'll bring him a plate later."

They started eating and conversation lagged a bit while they dug into the tasty meal. Geir was glad he had planned ahead. The steaks had come out very well and the side dishes complimented the meal nicely. He'd made a good showing for his first luncheon and he felt quite a bit of relief about it.

"So…Tibet?" Beau prompted after they'd had a chance to

enjoy their food for a couple of minutes.

"Yeah. Tibet," Geir repeated, trying to recover his train of thought. "They wanted me to stay on and teach, but a seer among the snowcat elders told me I had a different road to travel. My path was with the Nyx, she said. I offered myself to Ria as a Royal Guard and came up through the ranks to become Master when the old Master could no longer keep up with the duties. He died shortly after that, which caused great sadness to all of us who had trained under him. He was well loved and much missed. But it helped that I'd had his blessing to take his place. The *pantera noir* took me in at first for the sake of my aunt, but after the old Master named me his successor, they welcomed me on my own merits and I found my true calling, as the snowcat seer said I would."

And wasn't Geir just the gabby guy today? He almost didn't believe how many words were coming out of his mouth. Usually taciturn and silent, he had worried about being able to converse with his guests. Turns out, he needn't have worried after all. He was almost having a hard time shutting up. He decided he'd heard enough of his own voice for one meal.

"So, what are your plans?" Geir asked Jacki and Beau.

Beau gestured to Jacki, letting her speak first. "Well, the first thing I need to do is help Tom get better, but I decided to do that here because the High Priestess is coming here to train me. I'm going to join her order." Jacki's face flushed in the most charming way, almost as if she was embarrassed or excited—or both. "I never thought about being a priestess, but it feels right. Something happened during the battle…" her voice trailed off and Geir thought back to what she had done during the last battle in North Carolina.

"When you cast that amazingly powerful spell?" Geir prompted. "That was a masterwork of magic, milady. You saved the day and stunned all of those who saw it happen, myself included."

"Yeah," she agreed, sounding a little flustered, as if shy of what she had done. "That was when it happened. I was so scared, but yet…I felt more power flowing through me than I've ever felt before. I didn't understand what was happening. I'm still not really sure how it all occurred, but one minute I was praying and the next, the flow of magic came into me in a rush, allowing me to turn the tide on the evil spell. It was a really amazing feeling." She took a sip of her tea, her eyes still very distant in memory. "Bettina came to me a few days after and explained a few things. She also instructed me to come here. She said she'd arrive shortly to begin my training. She…uh…she wants to name me as her successor, though I still can't really see it."

"High Priestess?" Beau seemed as shocked as Geir was.

"If anyone has that kind of power, you do, Jacki. Don't doubt yourself. Few beings in this realm could have done what you did on that battlefield." Geir was used to giving small pep talks to his students who sometimes doubted their abilities. He was glad he knew what to say to take the uncertainty out of her eyes. She smiled at him and he felt like the sun had come out on a rainy day.

"Does Bettina plan on stepping down or something?" Beau asked, bringing them back to the practical.

"Not that I know of." Jacki bit her lip as worry seemed to return to her expression. "I think it's more that she's worried about what's coming. If she were to fall, she wants the succession to be secure, to avoid chaos in the leadership. I don't understand it all, but I decided back in North Carolina, before ever agreeing to come here, that I would do whatever I could to make this happen. Not for myself, but because I feel the same sense of dread about the future. I'm not a seer, but my aunt is, and she's offered quite a few warnings of late. And now, even the seas are forbidden to us because of the leviathan. It's not a good time to be a selkie and someone's got to take a stand against the evil that threatens us all."

Geir felt such pride in her in that moment. This was a woman of deep integrity. A mate he would be proud to call his own—if they were truly meant to be together—and one he would work to be worthy of for the rest of his life.

Jacki enjoyed having lunch with the two tigers, but in the back of her mind, worry set in. Tom wasn't getting any better. If anything, he seemed worse.

Back in North Carolina, during the battle, Tom had chosen to try to protect the small lake and had been overrun by the evil magic sent against them. Despite his enormous personal magical power, he had fallen.

When they had planned out their positions before the battle, Tom had relegated Jacki to the small stream that connected to the lake. He'd probably thought he could stop anything that might come their way before it got to her. She knew that Tom was trying to protect her, but only Jacki had known what her aunt, the seer, had told her.

Aunt Sophia had given Jacki very detailed, secret instructions about where she should be and when. Her aunt couldn't say what, exactly, would happen, but she insisted that Jacki—and Jacki alone—needed to be at that stream at the appointed hour. She had given Jacki very specific instructions not to tell anyone. Aunt Sophia knew as well as Jacki did that the men in their family had a noble, protective streak a mile wide. If Tom had known that Jacki was going to face the bulk of the danger, he would have been right there at her side. But their aunt had been adamant that Jacki had to face whatever would happen at the stream alone.

Jacki thought she understood now. By being on her own, she had reached out for help, praying to the Mother of All. And She had answered in the most amazing way. If Tom had been there, Jacki would have naturally pooled her magic with his and they would have tried to fight the evil alone. They would have tried and failed, and probably died, never calling on the Goddess, never receiving that miracle of Her intervention.

Jacki was coming to the realization that Tom had hidden the full extent of his injury from her—and from everyone— while they'd been in North Carolina. He had fallen under a *magical* attack, after all. Although he'd had superficial cuts and scrapes that had healed already, there was no evidence of what she suspected was a gaping, magical wound that could not have been treated by the doctors in North Carolina. No, the persistent wound that plagued Tom now was on a different plane. It was a wound to the soul. To the heart of his magical core.

And it had festered in the time since the battle.

She sat with him after lunch, trying to figure out what to do for him and worrying.

"Tommy," she fussed at him, her heart breaking as she sat by his bedside. "Why didn't you tell anyone? Why did you hide this?"

His deep brown eyes fluttered open. Seal eyes. His beast was very close to the surface.

"Didn't want you to worry, Twirp."

She gave him a teary chuckle at the use of her childhood nickname. Only Tommy had ever called her that.

"Well, you suck at that. I'm really worried now. What can I do to help you get better?" Her words were soft and filled with choked-back tears.

"Don't think there's much anyone can do. Just hold my hand little sis, and don't cry for me." His words trailed off and she took the hand he held out to her as his eyes closed.

She could feel him slipping away and the tears came, no matter his instructions not to cry.

A while later—it could have been moments or it could have been hours—Jacki felt warm hands descend on her shoulders. She looked up to find Beau behind her, his gaze on Tom's still face.

"What can I do to help?" Beau asked when he realized he had her attention.

"I don't know," she replied, helpless. She stood, placing Tom's hand gently at his side. He was unconscious again.

She made to move past Beau but he stopped her, his hands gentle on her arm.

"Hey now," he said softly. "Come here."

He opened his arms and she stepped into his embrace,

grateful for the small comfort as she leaned against his chest and cried silent tears of despair. Beau rocked her gently in his arms until she calmed, but she didn't move away. There was something so strong and safe about Beau's muscular arms around her. She felt protected in a way that wasn't threatening to her independence. She felt cherished. Almost…loved?

She looked up at him as the thought crossed her mind and was caught by his golden gaze. Time seemed to stand still as his head dipped, his mouth drawing slowly closer to hers.

And then he kissed her. Time stilled as the most gentle and respectful of kisses touched her lips. His warm, piney scent engulfed her, sparking something inside her that had lain dormant for a very long time. And then he rumbled against her. She broke the kiss, startled. Had he just…purred?

Jacki didn't know a lot about tigers, but she knew that if a lion shifter did that kind of thing—purring in human form—the consequences were pretty profound. As in *mating* profound.

Jacki couldn't handle this. She stepped away from Beau and headed for the door at a fast pace. She was thankful when he didn't follow. She was just a little too distraught right now to deal with any other majorly life changing experiences.

She fled through the house and found herself back in the large kitchen. Geir was still there, but she didn't really want to see anyone right now. The door to the back garden beckoned, but she couldn't be rude to her host.

He must've seen something in her expression because he stood and immediately came to her. He stood close and something within her wanted to lean on his strength. Surely someone who was a *Master* had enough inner peace to go around. She needed some of that right now.

"What's wrong?" His strong hands were gentle on her shoulders as he touched her. He was warm and comforting rather than intimidating, which was odd considering he was such a badass sensei. "Is it your brother?"

Mutely, she nodded, breaking down again. It was too much to bear. Tom had always been her rock, her solid ground. The one who bandaged her skinned knees and let her tag along on his adventures in the ocean and out of it. They'd been inseparable as children and had even maintained a reasonably close relationship during their rough teen years. Tom was older, but he never got too impatient with her hanging around, and she had idolized her brother most of their lives.

"I knew when I saw him get out of the van that something was very wrong with him," Geir admitted, rubbing her shoulders with a light touch. "Can anything be done?"

"I don't know. It's a magical injury, not a physical one. I'm hoping that when Bettina gets here, she'll be able to help him. Have you heard from her at all?" Somehow, Jacki's hands were placed flat against Geir's chest and she felt the reassuring beat of his heart. She didn't remove her hands, even after she realized the intimacy of the pose she had unconsciously adopted.

"No word yet, but Ria told me to expect her sometime today. Surely the High Priestess will be able to help him."

She knew Geir was trying to sound positive for her sake, but she heard the thread of doubt in his voice, no matter how hard he tried to hide it. She felt the same way and it all just became too much. She slid her hands up around his neck and rested her ear against the comforting beat of his heart, glad when his arms came around her somewhat hesitantly.

"I know what it's like," he said softly, surprising her.

"What what's like?" she whispered, not moving her head from his chest.

"To lose a brother by magical means," he replied, shocking her a bit. "I left Iceland because my older brother was killed by a mage. I don't think I ever want to go back to that cold, depressing country. Losing Thorson was almost more than I could stand."

She heard the deep, heart wrenching emotion in his voice, even though he spoke in tones hardly above a whisper. She got the feeling this was a secret he didn't share lightly.

"I would spare you that pain if it is within my power. If there is anything I can do to help you and your brother, I will do it. You don't even need to ask."

She lifted her head from his chest then and looked up into his icy blue eyes. She had thought them cold at first, but in truth there was a white-hot fire behind his gaze that warmed her, even as it enchanted her.

"I'm so sorry, Geir," she whispered, raising one hand to cup his stubbled cheek. She saw the devastation in his gaze as he thought about his lost brother, and his determination that she would not lose hers. Why he should care so deeply for her family was hard to fathom, but there was a sort of connection between them. Perhaps it had been forged in the battle when Geir had been the only one left standing to help them all get down the mountain. But it had been there even before—when she'd decided to trap him inside her final spell—a dome of protection that he wasn't able to break alone.

She had wanted to protect him. She had kept him from his duty to the Nyx, but somehow he had never chastised her for doing so. All she had known at that moment—low on energy and desperate to keep those she cared about from further harm—was that she must protect him too, regardless of how mad he would be at her later.

But he hadn't been mad. He had taken her, Beau, and her brother, to safety after the battle was over. He had also looked after them while helping with the logistics of mop up. He'd had duties to the Nyx and his fighters, but he'd always found time to check on her each day they'd been in North Carolina. When he'd left for New York, she had missed him and coming here today had been a bit like coming home, for some odd reason.

She found herself moving upward, reaching on tiptoe as his head moved downward. Their lips met in the middle, in a sweet kiss that turned suddenly hot. The gentle man turned into a wildcat in her arms and her body responded in kind.

This *so* wasn't the time for this, but by the same token…it totally was. She had wanted to kiss Geir for a long time, though she had never really acknowledged the thought until this very moment. He seemed as hot for her as she was for him, his mouth claiming and demanding, where she never would have guessed such passions ran beneath his calm exterior. He was fire in her arms rather than the ice he often portrayed, and she loved it. She loved that she could drive him to such an unpracticed, *real* response.

And then he had to go and wreck the whole thing…by purring.

Jacki broke away from his kiss and tore herself out of his arms. It was hard to do, but her mind was in turmoil once again. She had to find clarity. She had to *think*.

Seeing her opportunity, she fled through the kitchen door and took off through the back garden. The woods were beyond, and they were calling her name. She entered the thick forest, glad to know that Geir hadn't followed. At least not closely, if at all. She couldn't hear him at any rate. Which was good, she determined. She needed to be alone. She had to find some kind of equilibrium so she could deal with everything that had happened in such a short amount of time.

She felt a pull in the direction that led up the mountain and she followed it, not really caring where she was going. She just needed to wander a little bit, and this was as good a direction as any to go.

She should have been surprised, but wasn't really, about fifteen minutes later when she stepped into a clearing that held a small stone circle. And even more importantly, Bettina was in the center of it, looking for all the world as if she had been waiting for her.

Jacki felt an enormous sense of relief fill her being as she walked into the circle and went to Bettina, reaching out to her with both arms. Bettina took her hands and Jacki immediately felt a jolt of calm, pure energy reach out to her, stilling her inner turmoil a little bit.

"Thank goodness you're here," Jacki said with true feeling.

"You seem so conflicted, child." Bettina looked at her with concern. "I hope I haven't brought such chaos to your life."

"No, it's not you at all, milady. It's…" Jacki felt so stupid thinking about the two tigers and their reactions to her when her brother was so very ill. Her personal stuff could wait. Tom was so much more important. "My brother is very sick. He was injured in the battle at the lake, but it wasn't really a physical injury. He keeps losing strength and I'm afraid he's in a state I've never seen before. It's like a coma, but on the magical plane."

"Where is he?" Bettina was all business now, her fey eyes filled with unease.

"Back at the house. At Master Geir's house," she clarified. "We're all staying with him for the time being."

"Then there's not a moment to lose. Let's go see about your brother. Selkies are susceptible to many forms of magical attack, but if we catch it in time, we may be able to save him."

Her voice, as well as her words, were music to Jacki's ears. They took off the way she had come, walking briskly through the woods, not speaking much as they made haste back to the big old farmhouse.

CHAPTER FOUR

Beau had stayed to look after Tom when Jacki took off. Truth to tell, Beau was just a little too stunned to do much of anything after she left him. She was his mate. He had confirmation now. But she didn't seem all that happy about it.

He couldn't really blame her. Her brother was looking worse all the time and it was obvious she cared deeply about him. This wasn't exactly the time to be thinking about mating, but apparently the Mother Goddess had other plans. Beau wouldn't argue with the Mother of All's plan, but he could wonder at Her timing.

Beau could back off a bit, of course, if his inner tiger would let him, but in the end, he would claim her for his own. That thought gave him a bit of security and a sense of purpose. First though, he had to help her and her brother through this crisis. He didn't want to start off their life together with a tragedy. Beau vowed to do all in his power to help Tom recover, though he had no idea really, where to start.

Sitting with the guy was a small enough thing he could do, making sure Tom didn't get any worse while Jacki took a moment to regroup. If Beau was any judge, their reaction to each other had surprised her more than anything. She had looked really overwhelmed when she ran off, which was a bit of a relief, in one way.

If she had been overwhelmed, she had felt the same intense reaction he had. Right? That thought gave him comfort, even as his tiger demanded they go hunt her down.

He shushed the beast and did what the human side of his mind counseled—proceed with caution. Women were unpredictable in Beau's experience. He had to tread lightly, especially with a woman he fully intended to spend the rest of his life with. A little caution now might help them have a fantastic future. He could be patient. Somewhat. He'd do his best to tamp the cat's instincts down as much as he could, and do this the more human way. For now.

The door to Tom's bedroom opened with a small crash and Beau was instantly on his feet, ready and willing to defend the unconscious man in the bed. But it was Jacki, and she wasn't alone. A petite woman followed on her heels, and Geir was bringing up the rear, his brow furrowed in concern.

"How is he? Did he wake up at all?" Jacki asked Beau, her gaze on her brother as she took up a post at his bedside.

The other woman went to the other side of the bed and began checking Tom over with a professional air. Was she a doctor? She didn't look like any kind of doctor Beau had ever seen.

"No. Sorry. He's been out since you left," Beau reported.

"You stayed with him?" Jacki looked up at him as if he had committed some great act of kindness, but he didn't think it was that big a deal. He just nodded when her eyes welled with unshed tears and her mouth formed words of the thanks that she wasn't able to speak.

But he understood. In Beau's mind, Tom was important to Jacki, and Jacki was important to Beau, so it was only natural that he would help Tom. Even if Jacki didn't make Beau purr in human form, he would have hung around for Tom's sake. The selkie male was brave and had proven himself an able warrior. He was well worth helping for his own sake.

"This is bad," the small woman announced, then stood back, looking at the three others gathered around the bedside. "But I think we can save him. If we all work together. You two are tigers, right?"

Beau nodded, a little surprised by the woman's perception. Geir had come up beside Beau, and they both stood at the foot of the bed.

"She is the High Priestess, Bettina," Geir said softly, filling Beau in as the woman turned back to Tom, clucking and feeling his forehead and wrists.

Beau paused to nod his thanks at Geir. The High Priestess was rumored to be a powerful creature indeed. Beau had never seen her before, but he looked at the small woman with new respect. She was the chosen of the Goddess. If she couldn't save Tom, nobody could.

"Four elements, I think. I will stand for air, Jacki for water, of course." The High Priestess seemed to be thinking out loud. "Master Geir will be earth, and you, young man…" she looked right at Beau with those piercing blue eyes of hers, "…from all accounts, you have a volatile temper. In this case, that's a good thing. You will stand for fire." She looked around the room and then set her gaze on Geir. "Can this bed be moved out from the wall? It would be best if we could surround him."

Geir bent to grab the frame and Beau moved to help on the other side. As gently as possible, they slid the bed, Tom and all, out from the wall, positioning it in the center of the room as the High Priestess watched. She nodded in satisfaction when they had maneuvered the bed into the right place.

"Thank you," Bettina said briskly. "We'll do this first spell fast, to stabilize him and stop the decay. It will probably knock you all out for a few hours. You can rest tonight and then tomorrow we'll do something a lot more formal to start reversing this."

"What is it?" Jacki asked, fear clear in her tone.

"It's a kind of magical poisoning. I will teach you the signs to look for during your training, but your brother cannot wait right now, so let's do this quickly, to stop the drain on what remains of his power, then you and I can talk about what is to be done tomorrow. It would probably be best if you led the greater work, since you are his kin, but we can talk more later. For now, we're going to do a simple, but powerful, protective spell. We'll call on the four elements, combining our energies and binding Tom to us, here in this realm. It should block whatever is draining him and buy us time to figure out exactly how to stop it and reverse the process, if possible."

"If possible?" Jacki's voice rose in alarm.

Bettina smiled gently. "It might be possible to return what he lost, in which case he will recover quickly. It might not, in which case, his recovery will take longer as his personal power is restored bit by bit in the natural course of healing."

"Or he might not recover at all," Jacki said in a bleak tone and Bettina went to her, putting one arm around her shoulders.

"No, my dear. Don't think that way. We *will* fix this. We *will* save your brother. How could we fail with you and me, and two strapping young tigers to bind Tom here?"

Geir, the old fashioned bastard, dropped to one knee, his head bowed. "I pledge all my strength to you, High Priestess, and to you, Jacki." Geir looked up then, catching Jacki's gaze, and it looked like she brightened. He had given her hope. At least the dude had managed to do that much, and Beau had to grudgingly give respect where it was due.

Jacki reached out, taking Geir's hands in hers as he stood. "Thank you."

"Uh…" Beau felt the need to speak, but wasn't anywhere near as formal as Geir's gesture and words had been. "I'm in too. We'll fix Tom up. No problem."

Jacki reached out to touch Beau's arm, a small smile aimed in his direction as she met his gaze, thanking him too.

"Now that's settled…" The High Priestess sounded a little impatient, and the sense that there wasn't much time to lose took hold. "Master Geir, you take the north for earth—up above Tom's head. Angry man, you get the south, at his feet. Jacki, your water spirit goes to the west and I'm in the east for air. Now everybody join hands and say your prayers. I'll be drawing on your personal energies and those of the elements you represent during the ritual. Don't let go and don't fear. I know how much power you can spare and how much Tom needs. I'll strike a balance that we can all live with." She smiled, but Beau admitted to himself that he was a little frightened by the High Priestess.

She was a creature of myth and legend. She was mystical and incredibly magical. As a general rule, Beau wasn't all that comfortable around magic. It had caused some of the most painful moments in his life and he didn't really trust it—or those who depended on it.

His mother had been a priestess. She had lived her life with magic every day, and depended on it to her detriment. It was what had gotten her killed. And his father had died trying to protect his mate, leaving Beau all alone.

He just had to remind himself that this woman, this High Priestess, served the Goddess directly and there could be nothing evil in her or her actions. That was his only comfort as Bettina began chanting in a bell-like tone, her voice musical and full of magic.

Beau felt the magic gather as the little hairs on his arms rose. He felt a charge building in the air, like an electric current, but different somehow. The room got brighter and though there was no wind inside the house, a circulation of sorts began, sending a light show over the pale walls. It was like the aurora borealis met a disco ball as colors and light flashed and danced against the surface of the walls, and a golden glow began to form inside their circle of joined hands.

Beau felt the tingle where his hand met Jacki's, but on the other side, he felt the tug of the High Priestess's power as she drew on his energy. It was an odd sensation. It was like the link with Jacki fueled him and then it drained into the other woman, and from her, into the center of the circle—into Tom.

"Earth, air, fire and water, we stand against the darkness," Bettina's voice rose as she switched to English. "We stand against the forces of evil and the power that seeks to harm this man. He is our beloved brother and we are his protectors." The light and fury of Bettina's enhanced power rose to a crescendo and then descended over Tom, cocooning him in a golden glow that seemed to seep into his pores…and for just a moment…it lit him from within.

Colors continued to swirl around Tom like an aura for a few minutes as Bettina switched back to some foreign tongue Beau could not decipher. She was chanting softly as the power crested and then subsided, leaving his knees feeling like wet noodles.

The High Priestess let go of his hand and stepped back, her head dropping toward her chest for a moment as her eyes closed. Beau wasn't sure what he was supposed to do now, but sitting down sounded like a really good option. Falling down was a possibility. And passing out was also within the realm of probability. He felt truly awful. Drained. Wrung out like a wet dish rag.

Beau grasped the rail at the foot of Tom's bed with his free hand, using it to support him on one side as Jacki continued to hold his other hand. He noticed that she also still held one of Geir's hands, but surprisingly, his tiger didn't want to roar about it. Normally, the time between discovery of one's mate and the actual claiming, was rough. The slightest thing had been known to start terrible battles, and even a war or two, in ancient times.

At the very least, Beau had prepared himself for the idea that he might be a little overly possessive of Jacki until he could solidify the bond. Maybe being drained of most of his energy by the High Priestess had mellowed his reaction. If so, Beau was grateful for the reprieve. His father had warned him many times that Beau's unusually volatile temper could get him into serious trouble—especially when and if he finally found a mate.

Well, he'd found her now, but his temper wasn't riding

him the way it usually did. It was odd, really. Beau often had to work hard at keeping his temper in check. His family had gotten used to his quirks over the years, and they knew when not to poke the tiger. Most of his military colleagues had learned the same, though some had learned it the hard way. But now, when his temper should probably be the most out of control…it just…wasn't. In fact, he felt calmer now than he had in a long time. It was like just knowing that Jacki existed, and was here with him, was enough. Well…almost enough.

The tiger and the man both wanted to pounce on her and make love to her long into the night. They wanted to hole up in a room with her for days and try every position in the Kama Sutra—and some that hadn't been invented yet. But the tiger wasn't interested in biting Geir's hand off for daring to touch his mate…which really was decidedly odd.

"Are you two okay?" Jacki squeezed his hand as the High Priestess spoke, lifting her head.

"I'm okay," Beau answered, though his voice felt and sounded weak. Geir merely nodded. "How is Tom? Did we do it?"

Bettina bent over Tom to examine him. When she lifted one of his eyelids with her finger, Beau caught a glimpse of that same golden glow that had been around his body, now shining out through his eyes. Beau almost took a step back in surprise, but his legs still didn't want to cooperate with him.

Bettina rose and smiled. The older lady really did have a beautiful smile. Beau felt his heart lift, along with his mood.

"We've protected him well," she announced. "The drain on his personal power is stopped for now. He will get no worse before we have a chance to break the connection once and for all. You've all done very well. Thank you for your help and energy. I think the men should probably rest now, don't you, Jacki? Maybe you could help them find a place to sit. And you should probably stay with them for a little while, just to keep an eye on them. I'll sit with Tom and plan our next move. I'll meet you in the kitchen in an hour, all right?"

Bettina's smile invited no objection, but Beau figured Jacki probably needed a little break too. She looked a lot better than he felt, but he wanted to be certain she was feeling no ill effects from what they had just done before he let her go off with Bettina to plan more magic. If this was only a *small* spell, he almost hated to see what they would be doing tomorrow.

Geir walked out from behind the head of the bed and stumbled a bit. Jacki let go of his hand, which she had still been holding, and moved under his shoulder, putting her arm around him, supporting him. The two of them stepped closer to Beau, and he finally let go of the foot rail of Tom's bed, realizing too late that it had been holding him up.

Much to his chagrin, Jacki put her other arm around his waist and the three of them stumbled toward the door. Jacki was supporting the two males—one on either side of her womanly form. How embarrassing.

Geir tried to be prosaic about his own weakness, but the truth was he felt humiliated that Jacki had to hold him up. Beau too. They made slow progress down the hall and only got as far as the living room couch before all three of them collapsed onto the soft, overstuffed cushions. Luckily the thing was built on the large side and fit all of them comfortably. Geir didn't think he would be able to move under his own power anytime soon.

"I'm sorry, Jacki. Whatever you ladies did in there, it seems to have unmanned me," he admitted. "I feel like a kitten who's just been through a wild ride in a washing machine."

Beau laughed at that description. "Good one. I think I was on the same ride with you, Master G."

Geir wondered at the shortening of his name. Nobody had ever done that before and it felt…kind of nice. It was nice to know the other tiger felt comfortable enough to give Geir a nickname. Most others shifters were either afraid of him or in awe of his abilities. Few were comfortable in his presence and Geir had always found it difficult to make friends. The idea that Beau of the nasty temper was relaxed enough with him to shorten his name was surprising. And a little suspicious…

It had to mean something. But what?

Many strange and wondrous things had happened of late, and Geir had been trying to analyze events and make connections. Perhaps this was another of those strange and wondrous events that would come to mean something much more profound in the coming days? Geir didn't know, but it certainly was a small thing that meant a lot to him right now.

"He looked better, didn't he?" Jacki said, sitting between the men. Geir looked at her, seeing the fearful hope on her face. He reached down and took one of her hands in both of his, rubbing her soft skin with a light, hopefully comforting, touch.

"He did look better," Geir told her. "The glow of power you infused into his being agreed with him. Even I could see that."

"But will it be enough?" She bit her lip as she turned to look into his eyes and he couldn't help himself.

Geir bent and kissed her, tugging that poor, abused lip between his own, laving it with his tongue and then…taking the kiss deeper. His chest began to rumble and she pulled away.

The first thing he saw was Beau's murderous expression.

"What the hell do you think you're doing?" Beau's famous temper showed in the flare of his eyes, even if he was too weak to do much more than yell at Geir.

"It's not what you think. Didn't you hear the purr? She's my mate," Geir said lightly, feeling both wonder and pride in the words. To have a mate was a miracle. To have such a mate as Jacki, was an even more wondrous thing. She was amazing.

"She can't be your mate, G," Beau's tone was low and deadly, with a hint of the tiger in it, but he didn't scare Geir.

"Why not?" he challenged right back.

"Because she's my mate, dickhead."

"What?" Geir was nonplussed. How could this be? "I

don't get it."

Jacki stood abruptly, her turmoil clear in every line of her body. Her hands clenched at her sides, she turned to face them.

"I don't understand it either. I made you both purr and..." she trailed off, srunching her eyes closed as if she couldn't stand to look at them anymore. Geir fell silent.

"You did what now?" Beau demanded, apparently as confused as he was angry.

"I didn't do it on purpose!" She opened her eyes and pinned Beau with a look Geir was glad he wasn't on the other end of. She was pissed. And confused. "Here I thought lions were dense. Dammit, I didn't ask for any of this!" She spun on her heel and stormed out. Geir would have gone after her, but he couldn't move.

"Well, what the fuck?" Beau asked in a tired voice.

Geir looked over at his rival on the other end of the couch. He looked as bad as Geir felt. The drain of his energy was really hitting him now and unconsciousness seemed to be approaching rapidly.

"I'm sorry, Beau, but I won't give her up," Geir made his stance clear even as his eyes started to close.

"Neither will I, G-man, so we're going to have to beat the shit out of each other to find out who wins," Beau replied. "Tomorrow."

"Yeah. Tomorrow," Geir agreed, fading into the grayness that waited for him.

The next morning, Geir woke before his rival and left the living room. He stopped in his own room for a shower and a change of clothes, then headed out to find Jacki. The challenge would have to be settled before they could move on. Until the mate challenge was over, nothing else could proceed for either of the two men involved.

Ideally, Jacki could stop the challenge fight by simply stating her preference, but she was nowhere to be found. Neither was the High Priestess. Geir had looked in on Tom and found his condition unchanged. After that, Geir had made a quick search of the house and premises and couldn't locate either of the women.

He decided to go to the dojo and warm up before facing his rival. Geir wasn't foolish enough to underestimate his opponent. Beau was an experienced, professional soldier, who had years of combat experience. He would not be easily defeated. At least Geir hoped he would put up a damn good fight. Geir wanted a chance to pummel something— preferably Beau's face—to help work out some of his frustration with the entire situation.

Why couldn't something in his life go easily, just for once? Why must every last thing be a struggle? Something as profound and important as mating shouldn't be left up to chance—or the bloody battle that was about to ensue between two pretty evenly matched tiger shifters. The claws would be out and no holds barred.

Geir stretched his muscles, warming up in the dojo. He would be ready when Beau appeared. Wearing only the loose, but stretchy shorts he habitually trained in, Geir was as prepared as he was going to be when the door to the dojo opened and shut. Beau emerged out of the darkness by the doorway, dressed similarly. The brief outfit would allow them to change into the painful half-human, half-tiger battle form, or simply remain human. They could even go completely tiger and the shorts would probably go with them.

In the old days, these sorts of challenges were often done in the nude, but modern fabrics had allowed shifters at least some protection for their private parts when fighting on two legs. Their human skin was their most vulnerable form, and it was smart to protect the most vulnerable areas a little when they could.

"Have you seen her yet today?" Beau asked, his voice low, laced with rage as he stalked forward.

"No. She and the High Priestess were gone when I woke," Geir answered.

"Then I guess we do this. I won't give up my claim to

her," Beau nearly growled the words, and Geir felt the same way.

Geir studied his opponent. Beau's tiger was much closer to the surface than most. It would lend him its great strength even while in human form. This would be quite a battle.

Geir wasn't so conceited as to think that merely because he had earned the title of Master, that he could not be defeated. It was a teaching of his order that there was always someone or something cleverer than yourself. Conceit was the predecessor to defeat.

"I won't give her up either," Geir said firmly, standing opposite Beau on the matted floor.

The barn was huge and had been specially designed with a large, open, center area that was lined with mats, for just this purpose. A class of twenty would fit in the space comfortably. It would be more than adequate for a battle between two warriors.

There was no order to begin. There was no ritual bow. No words of commencement.

No, this was a battle of the oldest and most sacred kind. There were no real rules, except that each fighter follow his heart. If his heart demanded he fight for his mate, then he would do so to the best of his ability, using all his gifts and skills. If, however, his heart wasn't really interested in the woman in question, such a man would have a duty to withdraw.

Mating wasn't a game. It was a calling. A special bond gifted by the Goddess. One did not—and should not—take it lightly. It was serious business, with serious consequences for those who would meddle with fate.

Beau charged and Geir sidestepped, using Beau's momentum against him in a classic move. Had Beau been overcome by his baser instincts into making such a rookie move, or was he playing some deeper game? Was he testing Geir's instincts and reaction times? Or was he trying to lull Geir into overconfidence?

Geir was no green recruit to fall for such a trick. Instead

of waiting to see what Beau would pull next, Geir went on the offensive. He pushed Beau back, and back again, fists and feet flying in an acrobatic display. He threw some of his best moves at him, but Beau countered or avoided every one. Geir was impressed, but he hadn't shown Beau his full bag of tricks yet. Far from it.

The battle progressed, each man testing the other and getting in a few blows here and there. The surprising result, as the battle raged between them, was that they were pretty evenly matched. Geir was impressed again and again by Beau's creative moves and counterstrikes. He had a totally unique style that meshed well with Geir's own. If this situation weren't so serious, Geir would have wanted to pause and examine some of the lightning fast punches and kicks that came at him in innovative ways.

As it was, Geir was put through his paces, doing his best to keep from being clobbered or clawed. Yes, the claws had come out and soon, they would both test the limits of their endurance by shifting—or rather, half-shifting—into the more deadly battle form. Only the most skilled and powerful of warriors could hold the half-shift for longer than a few moments.

They had danced around each other enough. Geir called on his inner tiger and let the beast out just enough to gain several inches in height, sprout fur and claws and gain the strength of the tiger on top of his human strength. Battle form amplified power, allowing both creatures that shared the same soul to have access to the body at one time. It was painful, but it was also incredibly useful.

Both Geir and Beau were Alpha cats with no Clan of their own. They were loners. Members of a Clan through swearing fealty to another species' leader. They weren't leaders of their own Clans or Packs. They ran alone, though they had formed families of a sort with their brother soldiers. Geir felt like the brother or father figure, in some cases, to all those he had trained over the years. Beau undoubtedly had his own core group of friends he considered brothers and sisters. He most likely had a family somewhere. A mother, father...maybe some siblings, aunts, uncles, cousins.

All of those family—and pseudo-family—ties made one stronger. It cemented one's place in the hierarchy. It gave one status and comfort. It gave one purpose in life.

Alphas were the strongest of shifters, born to lead in whatever capacity fate chose for them. Some led Clans. Some led family units. Some led armies. And some led only themselves.

Geir was tired of being a loner. He was just tired of being alone. Period. He wanted a mate—this mate, the Mother of All had put in his path—more than anything in the world. He used that desire to help him hold his battle form longer than he had ever held it before.

Geir was a strong Alpha at the best of times, and he often trained his students using the battle form. He could hold it longer than any of those he had ever trained. But Beau was giving him a run for his money. Beau matched him. Step for step. Swipe for swipe. Claws clashed and slashed. Fur flew and blood spilled. And still they battled on...

They were both weakening, but stubbornly holding on. The first to lose the battle form would lose the girl, and Geir was very much afraid that Beau would not give in. Geir matched him, but he was starting to feel the strain in every fiber of his being. It wouldn't be long now before one of them struck a lucky blow that would kill.

Geir had never wanted it to go that far. In ancient times, and in less civilized areas of the world, mate challenges still ended in death, but it didn't have to be that way. One could win without killing the other. Geir had wanted a clean fight. One that didn't end in utter destruction, but there seemed no way around it now. They were too evenly matched. One would have to fall—and fall hard. Bad as he felt about it, no way was Geir going to let himself be the one to fail. This was too important. Jacki was too important. She was...everything.

"Stop!" A feminine voice filled with power sliced through the dojo only a split second before what felt like a lightning bolt crackled between Geir and Beau, knocking them both backward into the air, landing on their asses on either side of the dojo.

They both reverted to human form, bloody, but neither one of them beaten. They both looked at the women who had come in while they were fighting. Bettina was moving briskly forward while Jacki held back, watching with tears streaking down her face. Geir's heart clenched. He hadn't wanted to make her cry. He had never wanted that.

"I'm sorry, Jacki," he whispered, but she heard him. She looked at him and the tears kept falling silently down her beautiful face.

"Have you both satisfied yourselves that you are evenly matched?" Bettina asked in a stern voice. "I know you needed to do this, but really, couldn't you have figured it out a little sooner? You're both a bloody mess." She griped as she looked down at them. "Your challenge has ended in a draw. All fighting between you will cease. You will clean yourselves up and meet us back at the house in a half hour. Any shenanigans and I will personally kick your ass. Understood?"

She shook her finger at them both like some kind of school teacher, but Geir nodded and he saw Beau do the same. Nobody—not even two badass Alpha warriors—messed with the High Priestess.

CHAPTER FIVE

Bettina took Jacki's arm and pulled her along as she left the dojo. Geir wanted to talk to Jacki. To touch her and apologize for making her cry. He wanted to vow his undying love to her, but the priestess was taking her away.

Geir pushed to his feet, one goal in mind. He had to get cleaned up and go see Jacki. She needed him and he was messing about with Beau. His tiger was done with the fight. It had lost interest in pummeling Beau, which was odd in the extreme, if he stopped to think about it.

Geir wondered if Beau's famously bad temper had cooled. He looked cautiously at the other tiger shifter. Beau was pushing himself up off the mats, looking to be in as much pain as Geir was. Good. Geir didn't want to be the only one suffering. They had both beaten the shit out of each other. There was enough pain to go around.

"Still feel like killing me?" Geir asked tentatively as he stood facing his former opponent.

"Nah. I never wanted you dead, G. Just out of the way," Beau answered in a surprisingly calm voice. "Even my tiger doesn't want to see any more of your blood. That's a first."

"I know what you mean." Geir led Beau toward the front of the dojo where the locker rooms were located. "That has got to mean something, but I can't figure out what."

"Me neither." Beau scratched his head with a bloody hand. "But I bet the High Priestess knows. She's been messing with us since she got here."

"Agreed."

They hit the locker room, showering the blood off before each of them did a quick shift to full tiger form and then back again. Sometimes it helped heal minor wounds and speed healing of more...interesting ones as well. Nothing either of them had dished out to the other was too bad. It was as if they'd been going through the motions, testing each other's strengths and weaknesses, neither really wanting to kill the other.

Within the specified half hour, they presented themselves in the main house, only a little banged up from their endeavors. Jacki was pale and silent at Bettina's side. The High Priestess looked at them with a measuring gaze.

"I know all three of you are confused," she began. "Each of you men think that Jacki is your mate."

"I know she is," Beau declared loudly. Geir wanted to speak too, but the High Priestess held up both her hands, palms outward, quieting them.

"I don't doubt your claims. *Both* of your claims," she emphasized. "Have either of you bothered to consider how Jacki may feel?"

Beau looked pained while Geir just felt his heart sink. "I—" he started, then tried again. "I wondered if maybe it was different for her kind. I don't know much about selkies or how they mate. Though it pains me, I thought maybe she didn't feel the same."

"Oh, no," Jacki denied quickly in a raspy tone. "I never wanted to make you feel that way, Geir. Or you, Beau. I'm just..." She looked at Bettina. "I'm really confused. How can you both be my mate?"

"How can they not?" Bettina asked rhetorically, then smiled. "Jacki, you are going to be a priestess. Surely you must realize there is some precedent for a triad formed by two shifter males and a priestess."

"But we're not identical twins, or Lords," Beau pointed out unnecessarily.

"And I'm not Allie, destined to help her twin mates rule," Jacki added.

"Of course not, but Jacki, you will be in charge of something very important, if not rule, per se. After me, you will be the High Priestess."

"Only if you fall, you said," Jacki protested.

"Or if I retire," Bettina added with a benevolent nod of her head. "I've been High Priestess for a very long time. Even I might deserve a rest from my toils once this crisis ends. Don't you think?"

"It's not what I think that matters," Jacki answered, already showing the wisdom of a priestess, in Geir's view. "It's what the Lady asks of you and what you're willing to give."

Bettina nodded with a kind look on her face. "You're so right, my dear. And I have always given Her my all. But it's clear to me that even I may not live forever. Or work forever. There must be a successor, and the Mother of All has led me to you. Is it no wonder she wants you to have a strong and loyal support system should you need to fill my shoes?" She turned her gaze on the men. "And you two… You have both allied yourselves with Clans not of your species. Beau was drawn to the Kinkaids—one of the only tigers in their ranks. Why, Beau? What drew you there?"

Beau's face flushed, but he seemed resigned when he answered. "Jacki did."

"I did?" Jacki seemed truly surprised and very intrigued.

Beau nodded. "I saw you, and I knew I wanted to be near you. I thought at first it was just the magic of the selkies that attracted me, but I came to really care for your family. I would adopt Tom as my own brother, if I could. And I have watched you for a long time, wondering if maybe you were meant for me. I never had the guts to find out until now. You seemed so far above me… I'm just a simple soldier. You'll always be too good for me, Jacki, but I can't let you go. I can't give up the chance for happiness. I'll do everything I can to make you happy for the rest of your life, if you'll only be mine. I've loved you for a long time."

There was little doubt that Beau was embarrassed to have to declare himself in front of an audience, but Geir admired his courage in doing so. It was tough to hear that Beau had the prior claim on Jacki, having seen her first. But Geir wouldn't back down either. If what the High Priestess was saying held any merit, perhaps neither of them would have to back down. His tiger was already considering it. He could feel the cat watching and waiting to be consulted for its opinion.

"Master Geir, the *pantera noir* queen has your allegiance but you fought with the selkies in the last battle. Why?" Bettina asked shrewdly.

"It was my choice and my honor. The seer claimed that's where I needed to be, but I would have watched over Jacki and her brother, regardless. The moment I saw her, Jacki's spirit called to me. It was like a siren's song in the back of my mind. Irresistible and alluring. I needed to be by her side," Geir admitted. "My duty was to the Nyx, but I would have forsaken my oath if I'd had to. I'm not proud of that, but it's the truth. I had to be near you, Jacki."

"But you were so mad when I sealed you in the dome with us," Jacki said, bringing back the memory of that last battle.

"Mad at myself, mostly. I was fighting my instincts. I wanted to stay with you, but I knew my duty demanded I go help the Nyx. I thought you would be safely hidden without me, so I was willing to go, but then you turned the tables on me and sealed me in with you. It solved my problem because I had no choice, but I felt guilty for being so relieved that I wouldn't have to leave your side—and ashamed that I would consider forsaking my oath so easily."

"Mating goes above and beyond the oaths of men," Bettina reminded him. "Nothing can, or should, keep true mates apart. That is our Goddess's law. You need feel no shame, Master Geir. Your actions were honorable."

"So you're saying that we could both be mates to Jacki?

Like the Lords share their priestess mate?" Beau asked the question that was hanging out there in the middle of the room like the proverbial eight hundred pound gorilla.

"Yes," Bettina answered simply. "She will need your support as she learns her way into her new role as my successor. And if the day comes that she takes my place, she will need you both more than ever."

"But you have no mate," Jacki said, then cringed, probably realizing it might be a sore subject.

"I am not a shifter, dear. I did think I had found my mate once, many years ago, but it was not meant to be. Our love was forbidden and he…left. I have been as content as I can be alone, but as I say, I'm not a shifter. The way I do this job will differ from the way you'll do it, I'm sure. As a selkie, you are very magical indeed, but there are no shifters in this realm that can fully match my power. With one mate, you would be good, but with two strong Alphas backing you up, you will be much, much better." Bettina smiled. "If…you can figure out how to make this work."

"I don't even know where to start," Jacki admitted.

"That should be obvious," Bettina said, not unkindly. "You are all shifters. You should start with your animal sides. If they can't get along, your human halves don't stand a chance." Bettina's musical laughter filled the room.

That sage advice still ringing through his mind, Geir went for a prowl around the property with Beau, in their tiger forms an hour later. Geir had been wanting to check the perimeter he'd scouted the previous day, but he had been preoccupied with his guests until now.

Beau was a soldier. He had already proven he was as good as Geir in hand-to-hand combat. Geir was almost eager to see how Beau did out in the field, using some of the other skills Geir taught his students that he deemed necessary to be a Royal Guard. Tracking and scouting were right up there at the top of the list.

The two tiger shifters prowled the wooded perimeter of

the land that had belonged to the Millers, and was now Geir's new domain. They went right up to the set of cabins the Millers had kept for themselves in the real estate deal. Tad and Mandy's home, plus a cabin close to it that anyone in their family could use. The deal had been written in such a way that Tad and Mandy were precluded from selling their place to anyone other than Geir or the Nyx. If they chose to sell, or if their children or heirs chose to leave the mountain for good, their land would have to be reunited with the larger parcel the Millers had sold to Geir.

It was a friendly arrangement. Geir was content to have Millers and their kin on the land, but no strangers, and they had supported his idea to include that provision in the contract. As it was, Tad and Mandy had volunteered to be responsible for their part of the perimeter, which was low on the mountain, right up against a public road. But they also had made it clear that Geir was welcome to prowl there and send his scouts along the perimeter to check for breaches.

The Millers had a cub to protect, and they welcomed Geir and his students to help keep them all safe. By the same token, they didn't want to be the loose link in the chain that protected the Nyx. There was a long tradition of being Royal Guards in the Miller family, though they had always served the tiger monarchs. Still, they understood the value of the oaths Royal Guards—even the trainees—took, and the importance of dealing with anyone who would try to interfere with shifter monarchs in this troubled time.

So it was that Beau and Geir crossed over the boundary of the Miller place and found themselves very close to the public road. It wasn't much of a road. It didn't get a whole lot of traffic, but some of the locals used it as a shortcut from time to time—especially during heavy rain when the bigger road, lower down the slope, flooded.

The few local kids picked up the school bus each day from this road and that was about as exciting as the traffic on it ever got. Except for today…

Both Geir and Beau paused at the same moment.

Something smelled off. Old cigarette smoke wafted on the wind and the smell of oil and grease lay faintly on the ground. The tigers went instantly on alert. Beau started to track the scent as Geir played rear guard.

Keeping to the cover of trees, they found the spot where a car had paused on the shoulder of the dusty road. An oil stain could be easily seen several yards away. The vehicle was long gone, but Geir found it disturbing that it had stopped at all. The amount of oil indicated a slow leak and the amount of smoke odor hanging on the leaves meant the occupant of the vehicle had spent enough time here to smoke at least one, if not two entire cigarettes.

Shifters didn't smoke. At least not casually. It might occur in a ritual occasionally—especially among the more Native American species—but in general, it was very out of character. So who had stopped their car up here to smoke, and why?

This wasn't good. Beau became immediately suspicious of the vehicle and its smoking occupant. He didn't think it was more than one person. He could only see one set of tracks, but he would have to come back in human form to get a closer look. And he wanted to do that as soon as possible.

He turned back to Geir and jerked his head back in the direction of the house. Geir nodded, clearly understanding the gesture. They both loped off at a quick trot, breaking into a faster pace as soon as it was safe to do so. The sooner they got back to the road and checked things over, the better.

All the other shit that had happened today was immediately pushed to the back of Beau's mind. He'd been in a bit of turmoil since the big showdown with the ladies. Beau didn't know what to think about the idea of sharing Jacki with Geir. Frankly, he wasn't sure if he could.

While his tiger seemed okay with the idea—much to Beau's shock—his human side just couldn't wrap his head around it at the moment. Going furry and prowling the perimeter had seemed like a good thing to do to clear his head, but instead it had brought possible danger to their attention—which was also a good thing, if not exactly helpful with the mating conundrum. Ultimately, they needed to know if someone was watching them, even from a distance. Security was of the utmost importance.

Beau was a warrior first and foremost. A perimeter incursion was something he knew how to deal with. The emotional stuff was a lot harder.

They arrived back at the house and wasted no time shifting back to human and throwing on their clothes. Beau was glad they seemed to be on the same page about what had to be done. They didn't even need to speak much to know that they were both thinking the same thing, which was nice.

Geir grabbed some keys and threw a set to Beau. "The Millers had all kinds of useful things in the garages and barns that they couldn't take with them to Iceland," Geir explained on their way to one of the garages.

Beau whistled when he saw the well-stocked motor heaven. There were snowmobiles, a tractor, something that looked like an armored car, a couple of motorcycles and dirt bikes, and the vehicles they'd come for. Beau and Geir set out on four-wheelers moments later, heading for the road from a slightly different approach this time.

When they got near the spot the car had stopped, Beau used hand signals to tell Geir he would come in from the opposite side, just in case anyone was lying in wait. They worked well together, Beau had to admit. Geir was as skilled as Beau himself and, contrary to what Beau had previously thought, Geir knew very well how to use his skills in the field. He wasn't just a teacher. He could do the things he taught too. Beau was relieved.

It was good to have reliable backup. If they made a go of this strange mating idea Bettina had put forward, Beau just might find himself partnered with Geir in the field for the rest of his life. Now *that* was a daunting thought.

Beau had been a rolling stone for a long time. Since leaving the military, he'd been a mercenary, never staying long in one place, until he met Jacki. Only then had he decided to put down roots and swear himself to the lion Alpha of the Kinkaid Clan. He hadn't done it lightly. In fact, he had thought long and hard about it. He had even prayed about it, though he didn't go around talking about his faith in the Mother of All the way some shifters did.

He had a deep faith in the Lady and Her goodness. He always had. It was an intrinsic part of his nature that he didn't let other people see often, but it was there. His mother had been a priestess. She had taught him about the Goddess from an early age and he honored his mother's memory, carrying on the traditions she had taught him. He believed very deeply in the Mother of All his own mother had served faithfully, until her dying day.

Which was probably why he was even entertaining the idea of a threesome. Because the idea had been put forth by the High Priestess herself. A spiritual woman who had more experience with the Mother Goddess than anyone alive today. Bettina's words about how the priestess, Allie, was mate to the Lords and how Jacki was being groomed to take on Bettina's role had really hit home.

Jacki would need strong guardians at her back. She would be the next best thing to shifter royalty, but she wouldn't have the same advantages of a Royal Guard corps all her own. She would be a target, and she didn't have the same level of magical protections Bettina had. Somebody needed to watch Jacki's back.

Why not let it be Beau and Geir? The more Beau saw of the *pantera noir* Guard Master's skills, the more he realized Geir was more than worthy of the title of Master. He was probably a good teacher, but he was definitely highly skilled at applying the things he taught his people. The *pantera noir* Royal Guard had a badass reputation, and Beau knew from recent experience, it was well-deserved.

With Beau and Geir watching over her, Jacki would at least have two strong warriors to protect her. It would be hard for one man to do the job alone. Perhaps that's why the

Mother of All might be interceding in Jacki's case.

Beau still wasn't entirely sure that was really what was happening, but he was entertaining the idea. He would pray on it and see where his heart led him. If it was to Jacki's arms—and a threesome mating—well, he would have to get used to the idea, but it wasn't quite as abhorrent as he once would have thought.

He kept coming back to the thought of having two strong males to protect Jacki. She was going to be in increased danger just by virtue of the fact that she was going to be a priestess. Those sanctified women were always targets of evil because of what they represented, and what they meant to the communities they served.

Beau had seen first-hand how one man had failed to protect his priestess mate. It was one of Beau's most painful memories. His mother and father had died together, fighting evil, leaving Beau alone in the world. He had been an only child and after he lost his parents, he had lost his way for a long time. The military had given him some direction for his anger at the unfairness of life and the evil that tried to wipe out the few good things in it.

His mother had been purity and goodness itself. His father had been devoted to her. But it hadn't been enough. Evil had found them while they were away from home and all Beau had known was that they were dead and he was an orphan. He'd been old enough to go out on his own—seventeen—but he missed his parents to this very day.

Beau split off, heading for the opposite approach to the area where the car had been parked. They slowed the four-wheelers to check the ground as they came upon the scene. Beau found the tire tracks on his side and scanned them carefully without disturbing anything. He rode off to the side of the road, going slowly and looking at everything.

He met up with Geir on the spot where the car had stopped. And it was a car. He was certain of that now. The size, depth, and tread pattern of the tires belonged to a car, not a truck or van.

"Small hatchback, I'm thinking," Beau offered as they both studied what they could see of the tire tracks.

"Heavy load in the back of it," Geir agreed, pointing to the slightly deeper depressions where the back tires had been. "One person got out from the driver's side. Nobody got out any of the other doors. Might've been more people in it, but they weren't heavy, based on the track depth."

"Agreed," Beau said as he got off the four-wheeler. He followed alongside the set of footprints that led off toward the boundary. "Male. Maybe two hundred pounds. Smoker, obviously."

Geir joined him, walking on the other side of the tracks. "Wearing boots. About a size ten. Big guy," he observed, digging in his pocket for something. Beau was only mildly surprised when Geir pulled a plastic bag and a pair of plastic-wrapped, sterile, disposable tweezers from his pocket. A few feet away, he bent down and picked up a cigarette butt with the tweezers and placed it in the plastic bag. "No filter. Guy's hardcore. We might be able to get some DNA off this."

"You have access to a lab?" Beau was impressed.

"The Clan has many resources—especially when the safety of the Nyx is in question." Geir's blue eyes narrowed as he scanned the area once more. "I don't like this. What was he looking at?"

"Tad Miller's place is through those trees, but you can't really see the house from here," Beau stated, thinking through the options. "Our intruder stopped just before he would be visible from the house. How did he know?"

"He must've been here before," Geir stated the obvious. Both men growled in agreement that even the idea of some stranger prowling in their domain was not good.

Beau looked right and left, then right again. His gaze zeroed in on something shiny in a tree to his right, about fifteen feet up. "That camera is poorly placed. Even a human could spot it."

Geir looked in the direction Beau was pointing. "I'm not entirely sure that's one of ours." Geir looked concerned. "Let me call Tad and ask him to come out here. He knows this system inside and out. His father installed it and all the Miller cubs maintained it, according to what I was told when I bought the place."

Geir took his phone off his belt and punched a few buttons. He moved off to make the call while Beau investigated further. He found another camera in a rather odd position as well as some boot prints under a loose layer of leaves and other forest debris.

Beau was bent over an old print when Geir found him a minute later. "Tad's coming in through the trees. He'll be here in about two minutes."

"Watch where you step," Beau said, unnecessarily, as it turned out. Geir was stepping as lightly as Beau could hope for.

"What have you got?" Geir was instantly intent, looking over Beau's shoulder.

"More tracks. And look at the tree." Beau pointed upward at slight gouges in the trunk where someone had dug into the bark with metal cleats.

"These were placed recently and judging from the cleat marks, they weren't placed by shifters. What the hell is going on here?" Geir looked angry when Beau glanced up at him.

They both turned when they heard the snap of a twig, indicating they were no longer alone. Sure enough, Tad had arrived.

"Not yours, right?" Geir nodded toward the camera in the tree. They were too close to be seen by the wide angle lens at the moment.

"Never seen it before. Shoddy work. Too visible and too low to the ground. Ours are placed much higher and are a lot smaller. Better camouflaged too," Tad noted, concern furrowing his brows. "These are battery powered. They probably haven't been here long or one of us would've seen them. We're through here all the time."

"And yet, they've been here a few days at least. How old would you say these tracks are?" Geir pointed to the tracks that led right up to the tree.

"A week, maybe?" Tad opined after a careful examination of the tracks and the surrounding area.

"I agree," Geir commented with a nod. "But someone with the same boot size and tread was here today, a few yards from these camera placements. What do you think he was doing?" Geir's tone was contemplative. Not a teaching tone, exactly, but pretty close to it. Beau got a hint at what Geir was probably like when he was training new Guard candidates and was impressed.

"Might've been downloading any data on these units to a wireless device. They have short-range transmitters," Beau observed, having examined the unit from afar. "He'd have to get pretty close to download, then wipe the memory cards for a fresh set of images. He might have to come by once a week to get the images, then at some point, he'd probably have to replace the batteries in the camera units depending on how he has them set. They might be taking intermittent images, full-time video, or even motion-activated recording."

CHAPTER SIX

"We need to find out exactly what they're recording and how often," Tad said, his expression grim. "This is too close to my home and my cub."

"Agreed," Geir said.

He retrieved a set of gloves from his belt and quickly scaled the closer of the two trees that had cameras in them. He handled the device gently, switching it off first before doing anything else. Tad did the same for the other camera while Beau did a thorough search of the area.

Tad walked with them to where they'd left the four-wheelers. "I'll meet you down at the dojo," he said as they walked. "There are some things in that building I didn't have time to show you in detail. We have equipment to dust for fingerprints in the classroom and some other stuff that could be helpful."

"Good," Geir said, placing the camera gently on the seat of the vehicle while he rummaged around in the small compartment that held odds and ends. In particular, it had a wadded up plastic shopping bag that would help protect the cameras from smudging any potential evidence for the ride back up to the dojo. He and Tad placed the cameras into the bag and then Geir took off his shirt to use as a cushion inside the small compartment, laying the bag with the cameras on top and wrapping the fabric around it.

The ride back was slower because of the need to protect the cameras, but they still managed to get there before Tad had arrived. They had just put the four wheelers away and were walking toward the dojo when Tad pulled up on a dirt bike.

Over the next hour they discovered some of the hidden secrets of the dojo. There was the makings of a small crime lab in the room Tad had called a classroom, just off the main practice area, next to the locker rooms. No fingerprints had been found on the cameras, but they'd been able to determine that they were motion activated. It was easy enough to deduce that they had been reset after a recent download, and had been set to record fresh images.

That meant the driver of the vehicle had about one week's worth of surveillance of that part of the perimeter. The cameras would only have recorded when motion indicated something was in the field of view, so in all likelihood there would be a lot of images of birds and squirrels. But the really big potential problem was that there might also have been some snapshots of tigers caught on those downloaded images.

"We need to discover exactly who is watching the perimeter, why, and what they might have seen on the footage they've already managed to capture and download," Beau summed up as the three men sat back around the big lab table, grim expressions on their faces.

"The only good part of this is, with all the activity up on the mountain, we haven't had a lot of time to prowl in our fur this past week," Tad said. "The chances that he caught me or any of my family in tiger form on those cameras is lower than normal, but we'll have to check with everyone else who might've been patrolling the perimeter, to see if they remember going down that way over the past week or so."

"And there might be more cameras, on other parts of the perimeter," Geir added.

"Shit," Beau cursed, getting to his feet and pacing up and

down the room. "Why the fuck can't they leave us alone?"

The anger that usually rode him hard had dissipated since being in Jacki's presence these past few days, but it was never far from the surface. Beau was getting good and mad at the idea that someone was even now, stalking them. They had just fought a huge battle in North Carolina. Shouldn't they have at least a few days of peace before all this bullshit started up again?

"All right, let's make a plan," Geir said, getting them back to the point. He was good like that. He was methodical. A thinker. Beau found it helped him focus when Geir did his thing. "Tad, you know what to look for. Can you handle your part of the perimeter for now? Ideally, I'd like every section gone over by at least two different sets of eyes, but I have to brief the others first and I don't think we should wait that long."

Tad rose from his seat. "I'll do a sweep starting on the east side of my place and going west all the way around the mountain. I know these woods better than your people and I can move faster. I'll radio in when and if I find anything. Otherwise, I'll report as I clear each quadrant."

"I'll tell Ria and Jake what's going on and get some of the Royal Guard to do a second sweep. Nobody takes animal form until we're sure we don't have any more of those cameras," Geir stated as Tad agreed, then headed for the door.

Several hours later, it was determined they had already found the only two cameras on the property. Patrols had been stepped up on the perimeter and Ria was in the process of hiring some extra help from among those who had participated in the recent battle in North Carolina. She had made strong ties with the fox Clan of Mount Sterling Ridge and a team from Jesse Moore's mercenaries—known colloquially as the Ghost Squad. A few others had become trusted allies and when Ria called and offered some of them jobs, many responded that they would arrive ASAP.

Until then, Geir had worked out a stepped up rotation among the Guards and others who could help. A technical expert had been found among the group who was able to recover some of the downloaded data from the memory chips of the cameras. It seemed that once the information was downloaded and set to record over the old data, the old images were still available—if you knew how to get them—as long as they hadn't been recorded over yet.

They were able to recover over ninety percent of what had been downloaded and Jake was in the process of reviewing it up at the main house. So far, there were a lot of stray squirrels and birds, as Beau had expected, but Jake was watching a couple of hours of images for the possibility that a shifter might have gotten caught on those cameras unaware.

As the sun started to sink low on the horizon, Beau realized he hadn't seen Jacki or Bettina all day. He supposed they were together, starting Jacki's training or something, but he found he missed her presence. He had been doing important work to help protect her, but he always felt better when he could see her and knew she was safe. Too much time had passed since he'd seen her. His tiger was getting anxious. He felt it itch just below his skin.

"I think that's all we can do for now," Geir said, sitting back. They had been in the classroom and lab most of the day, using it as a sort of command center to centralize the effort.

"I want to find Jacki," Beau admitted, surprising himself with his candor.

"She's with Bettina," Geir confirmed Beau's guess, then stood up and stretched. "But I agree. Let's go find her."

It didn't take long. Beau was a little surprised to find Mandy Miller and her cub sitting watch over Tom's inert body, her fingers flying over her laptop computer as she sat at his bedside. Her little girl was playing with a few toys near her feet. Mandy looked up from her work when Beau looked into the room and smiled.

"Bettina asked if I would look after him while she and

Jacki went for a walk," she explained.

"That's kind of you," Beau said, not really knowing how to respond. He didn't know much about the woman. She seemed to guess the line of his thoughts because she explained.

"Tad and I both went to medical school with Gina, the tiger princess, and our folks were Royal Guard. Heck, we were Royal Guard from the time we were both teenagers. We guarded Gina all through school and even after. Plus, Tad wanted me and our little kitten—" she reached down and stroked the toddler's hair with affection, "—farther inside the property line after discovering those cameras on our land. I agreed."

"You're welcome to stay here for as long as you need," Geir offered, poking his head into the room.

"Thank you, Master Geir," Mandy smiled brightly at him. "We may take you up on that, depending on what you've discovered about the cameras. Tad and I can watch Tom for you tonight, if you want a break. As I said, we're both trained medical professionals. When Gina decided to go to medical school, a bunch of us did the same so we could keep an eye on her."

"Now that's dedication," Beau quipped, smiling.

"It wasn't that bad. If you ever met Gina, you'd understand why it was so easy to follow where she led—even to impossibly hard schoolwork and exams. She's very special."

"I've never met the tiger princess," Beau replied, somewhat wistfully. He hadn't really associated with other tigers since his parents' deaths.

"Well, stick around with this crowd long enough, and I'm sure you will." Mandy gave him a smile. "If I had to guess which direction the priestesses went, I'd suggest you try northeast. There's a stone circle up the mountain a ways."

"Thank you, Mandy," Geir said formally. "And thank you for watching Tom."

She waved away his thanks with a smile and went back to

her laptop while Beau followed Geir out of the room.

Once they determined the women weren't in the main house, the men set off through the woods, following their trail. Since the ladies hadn't been hiding their tracks, it was easy enough to find they had indeed spent some time in the stone circle Mandy had mentioned. From there, the paths diverged. Bettina had gone toward the Nyx's house, even higher up on the mountain, while Jacki's scent had veered off in another direction.

Jacki was glad to find the small mountain lake about a quarter mile from the stone circle. It was smaller than the one in North Carolina, and so far, the taint of evil wasn't very strong in its waters, but that could change rapidly now that the evil *Venifucus* had called a leviathan out of the deep. With it had come a host of other evil creatures that made their homes in the oceans, rivers and lakes. It was so bad now that Sam Kinkaid, leader of the Clan that bore his name, had sent out advisories to all the selkie members of his Clan and to his contacts around the world, advising a total boycott of the oceans and larger bodies of water for the time being.

Seers—including those in the powerful Kinkaid Clan, and the Nyx's new mate, Jake—had promised that the threat would be dealt with, but the time had not yet come. In the meantime, the safest place was out of the water. That was really hard for a selkie. Half of Jacki's being craved the water and its freedoms.

Even a small mountain lake could be a form of respite for her wild side, but until it was clear of the threat of evil, she couldn't chance it. Bettina had sent her here though—on a mission. Bettina had asked her to purify the water here using the same skills she had used in battle in North Carolina. Only this time, it wouldn't be under stressful conditions. This time, Bettina wanted her to pay very close attention to the power she called on and how it worked through her.

Jacki had spent long moments thinking and then praying, calling on the Mother of All to help her clear the taint of evil that had only just started to take root in this idyllic place. Jacki looked at every detail as the power came to her and worked through her, purifying the small lake and blessing each and every one of the small creatures that lived within. The Mother of All was Mother Earth in that moment, blessing Her creatures and shining Her Light into the depths, cleansing them, using Jacki to direct the power.

Jacki realized she was the conduit for the Goddess's energy. Jacki was the servant through which the Goddess worked on this plane of existence. Jacki smiled with joy as she felt the approval of the Mother Goddess, and Jacki learned the lesson Bettina had set for her.

When it was over, Jacki fell to her knees, tears of joy sliding unheeded down her face, her hands still outstretched as they had been when the Lady's power ran through her being. She was a bit drained, but nothing like the exhaustion she had felt after the battle in North Carolina. She had learned a great deal today.

"Are you okay?" Beau's voice came to her just before she felt his arms settle under hers, lifting her to her feet. He leaned her back against his chest, taking her weight as if she was going to fall over without his support.

She laughed at his caution. "I'm fine. Just a little overwhelmed at the moment."

Geir stepped in front of her, a frown marring his handsome face. "Should you be this close to the water?"

They had all seen the evil that had been conjured in another lake, down in North Carolina. These men knew first-hand what danger might lay in the water nowadays.

"It's safe now." Jacki claimed with a feeling of pride. "I purified it with the Goddess's energy."

"As you did once before." Geir nodded as they all remembered that last battle.

"Yes," she agreed. "Only this time, I actually knew what was going on and was able to learn a great deal. Bettina set me this task and now that it's done, I don't know about you two, but I'm going for a swim."

As she said the words, she began to shuck her clothing. Shifters weren't generally shy about their bodies, but Jacki had never been quite so out-in-the-open about getting naked in front of males she was attracted to. For one thing, in her own Clan, she was surrounded mostly by lions. Those women were tall and thin, muscular and svelte. Only among the few selkie shifters had Jacki felt comfortable, but even then, she was always a tiny bit rounder than the others.

She had big hips. At times, among the other skinny-bitch lionesses, she'd felt like her hips weren't just big, but massive. And she had big breasts. Not that any males had ever complained about that particular feature, but she was quite different from her lion relatives in the Clan. And that had made her self-conscious in a way that most shifters weren't.

Much to her surprise though, she found she didn't care at the moment, if Beau and Geir saw her before she made it into the cover of the water. The magic flowing through her had taken away some of her inhibitions and her usual shyness. Her beast was calling to her. It had been too long since she'd taken her alternate form. The water was pure and sparkling—whispering to her animal heart. Jacki stripped fast and walked straight into the water, allowing the change to come over her until she could dive cleanly under the surface in her seal form.

Heaven. Pure, unadulterated heaven.

Jacki swam the perimeter of the lake, nosing around rocks and discovering all there was to see in this new place. Her seal was full of curiosity about the place, the types of fish and the size of them. Much to her delight, there were some very large, tasty fish that she could easily catch for supper. She snagged one in her mouth and surfaced to throw it onto the bank.

While she would enjoy the fish raw either in her animal form or as sushi, she thought maybe for tonight, she would share her catch with the men, cooking them back at the house. Then she remembered Tad and Mandy would probably still be there, and she turned back to look for a few more fish.

What she found instead were two golden tigers, paddling happily toward her. She felt joy in her heart, seeing how much the big cats seemed to enjoy the water. They definitely had that in common with her. She wondered for a moment what they thought of her alternate form. Seals weren't quite as glamorous as furry, striped, fierce tigers, but she had her talents.

She dove under the water, determined to show them at least some of her skills as she swam loops around the men. She would hit them with a flipper now and again in a soundless game of tag that they could not win. But they didn't seem to mind. They played with her, splashing and frolicking like kittens to her seal pup, until all three of them were played out.

Just then, she saw a big fat fish swim by and she grabbed it with her teeth, slinging it onto the bank with the other she had caught before. The tigers, seeing this, were not to be outdone. Suddenly a fierce fishing battle was on as each of the cats began to stalk through the shallows until they had a nicely rounded pile of freshly caught fish heaped on the bank.

Jacki felt more at peace than she had in a long time. She shifted shape as she exited the water, letting it sluice off her skin as she headed for the grassy bank. She heard the tigers go quiet behind her and knew they were watching her as she lay down on the soft grass, letting the sun dry her skin.

The residual power of the Goddess still pulsed through her body, making her feel good in a purely feminine way. Forgotten were her worries over her size and shape. The hungry regard of the two very naked men who came to stand over her made her conscious only of them and the undeniable attraction pulsing between her and them. She forgot all her insecurities in the heat of their gazes.

Geir was on her left, Beau on her right. She shaded her eyes to look up at them, noting that both were hard and ready…and oddly, not fighting for dominance over her, or especially over each other. That was rare for shifter Alphas. It was unusual that two males who were unrelated got along so well when mating was in question.

Mating disputes, while they rarely occurred, often ended in bloodshed, sometimes death, so this was something remarkable indeed. Remarkable too was the sheer size and beauty of the two males. They were big tigers—a race she had only been exposed to recently. Many of her relatives were lion shifters. She was used to big cats, but tigers were a little bit different from her king-of-the-jungle relatives.

For one thing, she found them sexier. Those stripes and the slinky way they moved made her want to pet them. Or maybe it wasn't every tiger that made her want to do such things. Maybe it was just these two, very special tigers.

"Lay with me," she whispered up at them. "Let the sun dry us before we have to go back." The power of the Goddess was slowly leaving her, making her feel languid and a little lazy. Or maybe it was more fatigue than anything else, but either way, she just wanted to lay there for a little while, her men beside her.

And when had she started thinking of them as *her men?* Oh, dear. Was she really seriously considering the threesome Bettina had talked about? Were *they* considering it? She looked from one to the other as they sank down to the soft grass on either side of her. Were they even capable of such a thing? All the signs so far indicated that they might be. But did Jacki dare to ask it of them? It would be a sacrifice for them—sharing a mate instead of having one woman all to themselves.

If they went through with this, she felt like she would definitely be getting away with something. Two strong males to see to her every desire. Two to protect her and cherish her and make babies with her. Two mates to love and cherish back. Did she dare?

Jacki was still very confused about the whole thing, but she was willing to suspend judgment right now and just go with the flow for a little while. Bettina had advised that she see where things led before worrying the situation to death, and Jacki vowed to do her best to follow that advice.

She reached for their hands—one on each side of her. They were close, but they weren't quite touching. She appreciated the patience and care they displayed for her person. Many male shifters went on the attack when they saw a woman they wanted. Especially if she was naked. These two knew somehow that a show of aggression wasn't the way to win her. Selkies were more subtle than that—and Jacki in particular, needed more than that.

She was a woman of power in her own right. She needed to be wooed.

CHAPTER SEVEN

"I think that worked out pretty well," Beau said, drawing her attention, though he seemed to be looking at the sky and contemplating the movement of the leaves on the trees. "I mean, our beasts all seemed to get along. Don't you think?"

Geir rose to his elbow and looked at her and then at Beau. "You're right." He seemed a little shocked. "At no time did I want to rip your head off."

Jacki laughed at his rather bald statement though it was clear Geir hadn't meant it as a joke. Beau smiled too, though he didn't laugh outright. English wasn't Geir's first language and sometimes his foreignness came through in unexpectedly humorous ways, she was learning, much to her delight.

"Our cats seem to think they're evenly matched," Beau confirmed. "And they like the seal too. My cat thinks she's cute and is a little envious of her skill in the water. My tiger loves the water, you know." Beau leered a little at her, in a comical way that made her giggle.

"That was duly noted when you joined the Clan, Beau." She remembered the way Beau had bested some of the Clan's lions in the water, much to their chagrin.

"You have dealt with seals before, right Beau? Is this lack of aggression normal?" Geir asked, seeming intrigued.

"Not normal at all," Beau admitted. "Much as I like them,

my cat is always tempted to hunt. I mean, *always*. I fight my instincts all the time when I'm in the water with them. Thankfully, even if I lost control, they are way better swimmers than I am. I felt secure knowing they can outmaneuver me on any given day."

Jacki was surprised. "I had no idea," she admitted.

"That was the point. I didn't want to get thrown out of the Clan because I have a little aggression issue. I've been this way all my life. I have more than my share of the animal in my soul. The tiger is at the forefront most of the time, even when I'm in my human form. I know it's not like that for everyone, but for me...it's a way of life." Beau looked away as if admitting his affliction was something shameful. Jacki squeezed his hand. "But I handled it better when I was around you, Jacki. That's part of the reason I finally decided to stop roaming and take the position offered to me in the Kinkaid Clan. It was to be near you."

"Because I tame the beast within you?" she asked, needing to know if that was the only reason he had joined her Clan.

"For that, yes," he replied, looking deep into her eyes. "But also because I just...like you. I like being near you. I like hearing you laugh and you..." He seemed to be having a hard time admitting all these things, but Jacki felt like he was giving her the moon. "You make me happy, Jacki. Happiness has been in very short supply in my life."

"Oh, Beau," Jacki whispered, turning to him and letting go of Geir's hand.

She touched Beau's face, cupping his cheek with her palm as he rose off the ground to meet her. His lips covered hers in a soft kiss that quickly grew. Their bodies were slick with residual water from their swim and when she felt his chest rub against her bare breasts, she squirmed against him, wanting more. She felt the rumble of his purr against her chest and it made her move back, breaking the kiss.

Suddenly she remembered they weren't alone. She looked to her left, but Geir was on his feet, his clothing in his hand as he walked away from them.

"I'm sorry," she whispered, meaning it for both men.

Beau let her go and sat up, resting his head in his hands for a moment, as he bent over his upraised knees. He looked pained. As pained as she felt, watching one of her tigers walk away. Jacki got to her feet.

"Geir, wait..." She went after him, grabbing her clothing off the ground as she went.

She hopped her way into her pants, then threw her shirt over her head as she walked along, sticking her underwear in her pockets. He had paused to step into his pants, allowing her to catch up to him.

"I'm sorry, Geir," she repeated softly.

"No need to apologize," he said in a resigned voice. "It's clear that our beasts get along, but the human part of me isn't ready to deal with this yet."

He stood, buttoning and zipping his jeans, his muscular chest gleaming in the sun. He was powerfully built and Jacki wasn't unaffected by the sight of him.

"If it's any consolation, I'm really confused," she admitted. "I have feelings—strong feelings—for both of you. I'm sorry we've all been put in such a strange position, and I'm not sure what to do about it or how to proceed."

"One step at a time, I suspect," Beau said, coming up behind her.

She glanced back at him to find he was wearing his pants, his shirt held in one hand. She was surrounded by shirtless, hunky men, but they were all a little too on edge to do anything about it. Or were they?

Beau was at her back, slowly pushing her forward with gentle pressure until she stood very close to Geir. He hadn't moved. His head had quirked to one side as if in question, or some of the confusion she was feeling.

She lifted her hands and placed them against his chest, feeling the racing beat of his heart. He wasn't as unaffected as he appeared on the outside. She moved her hands, stroking him as she stepped closer. Beau stayed where he was, about a foot or two from them, still close enough that she could feel his warmth against her back, but allowing her the freedom to choose her next move.

She chose to kiss Geir. Rising up on her toes, she sought his lips with her own. She initiated a sweet kiss, but Geir soon turned it into a sultry assault on her senses. Still waters ran very deep with this man and she felt the hardness of his chest against her—the thin fabric of her shirt not much of a barrier as she lifted her arms to twine about his neck, sinking her fingers into his short blonde hair.

When he began to purr, she didn't pull back. She was coming to expect that low rumble against her chest and it felt welcoming and really, really sexy. The kiss turned molten and she almost stumbled backward with the force of Geir's passionate assault, but Beau was there. He caught her with his hands at her waist, his strong chest against her back.

A little growl behind her and the thrumming of Geir's purr against her front made for a heady mixture of sensations. She didn't squawk when Beau's hands lifted her shirt upward, skimming it off over her head as Geir let her mouth go for a few milliseconds. And then Beau's hands were on her skin and Geir's mouth moved to her neck…and then downward.

Beau pushed his hands into her pants—one in front and one behind—while Geir's mouth found her breasts. She squealed then, a high-pitched tone that rang through the empty forest like a bell of delight, when Geir sucked on her nipple. Her hands were in his hair, mussing the blonde locks that were usually so perfectly groomed.

She liked him wild. She loved the way he was learning what she liked. And she about died when his teeth scraped along the side of her breast, his tongue laving the hard center while his fingers toyed with the other one.

And then Beau's fingers slipped into her folds. One hand found her clit, the other found its way over her ass, gripping and squeezing. Sweet Mother of All, that was exactly what she needed to send her into orbit. Two men. Four hands. Two mouths—for Beau had bent to nip at her neck and nibble on her earlobe.

Jacki came when Beau's finger dipped into her core, sliding in the slick fluid that he and Geir had brought forth with their sensual moves. Geir pulled back, looking down into her dazed eyes as she came, his hands on her breasts, his gaze searching hers. He seemed surprised to find them all in this intimate situation…but not displeased. He looked over her shoulder at Beau and instead of anger, he seemed to be excited, which made Jacki even more so.

"Are you inside her?" Geir asked Beau point blank.

"Oh, yeah," came the rumbling reply from behind her. She just knew the damned cat was smiling as he stroked his finger in and out of her tight hole. The angle was tough and her pants, though stretchy, were impeding his movements, but he was adept at what he was doing. "She's hot, wet and tight. She's going to be so good when we get her someplace we can do this right."

That made them all still. Jacki leaned back against Beau, twisting her head backward so she could see him. But it was Geir who spoke.

"Are we?" he asked starkly. "Are we going to do this? The three of us?"

Beau removed his hands gently from her body, then slipped them out of her pants with a gusty sigh. He bent to retrieve her shirt and shook it out before getting ready to help her slip it over her head.

"I honestly don't know," Beau finally answered as he lowered the shirt over her torso. "But that was one of the hottest things I've ever done. Maybe there is something to this weird trio idea after all. I actually liked watching you pleasure our girl. How was it for you, Jacki?"

She knew she was blushing, but she held her ground. It would never do to show any sort of weakness to these two predators, even if they were her sworn protectors. A girl had a reputation to maintain, after all.

"I liked it," she admitted softly, unwilling to say much more until she had a chance to calm down and think things through.

"I'd say you did more than like it." Beau caught her eye as he licked his fingers with a lascivious grin.

She realized he was tasting her on his fingers and she felt her face flame, as did her passions. She would drop to the ground and spread her legs right now if he crooked his finger. She was only partially satisfied by the little climax they had given her. The small pleasure only made her crave more.

"What about you, G-man?" Beau gave her a break and turned to ask the other man.

"I…" His gaze narrowed on Beau's fingers, now licked clean. "My cat wants to taste some of that cream."

Jacki's knees quaked at the growl in his voice. Geir, who was always so controlled and calm. He was letting his wild nature show in the most delicious way. She wouldn't forget the way he'd used his teeth on her—gentle, yet exciting. It was unexpected from the usually solemn man…and strangely endearing.

As was Beau's gentleness. She would have expected it to be the other way around. Beau's famous temper had made her think he'd be a wildcat in the sack, but it looked like things would prove to be a little reversed with these two exciting men.

"Next time, brother…" Beau promised Geir, "…you can do the honors."

There was no question about it. These two were going to be the death of her…in the most scandalous, delicious sense.

"If there is a next time," Geir said, redirecting his gaze to Jacki.

But she was too confused right now to think. She wanted to defer the serious part of this discussion until she'd had time to sort through her feelings calmly and think about all possible consequences of this situation.

"We've been away from the house too long. I want to check on Tom and we all need something to eat." She looked back toward the lake. "We should probably bring those fish along and fry them up for dinner. We can talk after we've had a chance to freshen up, okay?"

Why did she think the men—both of them—looked disappointed with her dodge? She turned away, hustling over to pick up the fish, but the men followed her and Geir simply nudged her gently out of the way, using his discarded shirt as a make-shift carrier for the pile of fish. Beau helped him load up the fabric and roll it into a manageable ball with the fish inside and the ends secured.

She watched them work silently, only just realizing how well matched they were. They seemed to work together like men who had been friends for years rather than having only just met recently. Was it because they were both tigers? Both Alphas? Or both warriors?

She wasn't sure what caused the rather obvious connection between them, but it was good to see. If they did proceed with this threesome, the men would need that common ground to get along in such close proximity.

Mandy had been wonderful, staying with Tom while they were gone. She and her husband had moved into a guest room on the second floor, even though Geir hadn't yet gotten to those rooms with his remodeling plans. Perhaps that was why they felt more comfortable up there. That part of the house was exactly as their parents had left it.

Tad helped clean the fish and they all had dinner together as the men grilled their catch. It was a pleasant enough evening, even if Tom was still out of it. His condition worried Jacki, but she knew Bettina would be back later that night, when the moon came out, to help him again.

By the time the moon rose over the trees, dinner was long over and everyone had had a chance to clean up in preparation for the night's magic-working. Jacki was surprised to find that Bettina had asked Tad and Mandy to participate in the evening's work as they all reconvened in Tom's room, awaiting Bettina's arrival back at the house.

Jacki hadn't had a moment alone with either of the men, so she had been able to defer any deeper discussion of their situation. She was hoping they would have a chance to talk after they helped Tom, if they weren't all exhausted from the spellcrafting.

Bettina swept into the room in her usual whirlwind, catching them all up in her enthusiasm and bustle. She arranged them quickly around Tom, and began chanting the words she had taught to Jacki that afternoon. This time, Jacki and Bettina held hands over Tom's still form, one of each of their hands holding one of his. Tad and Mandy were behind Bettina, one of their hands on each of her shoulders. Beau and Geir were behind Jacki, in the same pose.

Jacki could feel the power build as Bettina guided it into Tom, to begin his healing. She reinforced the barrier that kept the evil from draining him further, then set about working her magic on his internal, magical wounds, strengthening him from the inside out. She worked slowly and surely, letting Jacki watch every step, learning as she went.

Toward the end of the working, Bettina encouraged Jacki to try to wield the power herself with good results. Jacki was able to do a bit of the healing—not as much as Bettina had accomplished—but still quite a bit more than Jacki had expected she would be able to do.

When they were finally done for the evening, everyone was drained, but Jacki most of all. Tad and Mandy disappeared into their room while Bettina instructed Geir and Beau to take Jacki to her bed. The High Priestess promised to look after Tom, who was resting more easily. He looked better, but Jacki knew as she was carried out of the room in Beau's strong arms, that they still had work to do to heal her brother completely.

When she woke sometime later, Jacki realized a few things simultaneously. First, she was naked and in her bed, in her room. Second, Beau was also in the king sized bed, also naked, sleeping on her right side. And third, Geir was on her left, also naked if the warm, rough skin rubbing against her leg was any indication.

How had they gone from the confusion at the lake to this? Jacki felt like she was missing something important here, but she'd been too tired from the spellwork last night—however long ago that had been—to pay too much attention to how she had gotten here.

"You awake?" Beau asked in a sexy, growly, sleepy voice.

"Yeah," she whispered back. She felt Geir stir on her left, rising up on one elbow to look down at her.

"We had a talk last night," Geir said without preamble. "Beau and I."

"You did?" She was almost afraid to hear what they had talked about.

"Yeah," Beau replied, her gaze sliding to him. "We decided to stay with you to see how this might work. You were too out of it to get your opinion on the idea. Sorry." He didn't look sorry in the least.

"We will leave the moment you ask it of us, but after what happened at the lake, both of us thought maybe there was some merit to the High Priestess's idea, and that we should explore it further—if you are willing, of course," Geir explained. His earnest expression and rushed words endeared him to her even more. How could she deny these men anything they asked of her?

She had deep feelings for them both, but the idea of having them—both of them—in her life in a permanent, sexual way...it was mindboggling. She had never had any expectation of attracting more than one man. Frankly, she had despaired of ever meeting the one man meant for her. Sometimes shifters went all their lives without finding their true mate and she had half-expected she would be one of those unlucky souls.

And then here she was, with *two* men who could be her true mates. It was nearly unthinkable. Except...here they were. Two tigers, going against their normal animal instincts to compete for a chance to mate. In fact, they both claimed their beasts were okay with the arrangement. It was the human side that balked.

For Jacki too. Her animal side didn't care. The seal didn't mind that the men were tigers or that there were two of them. The seal side didn't care that both wanted to pleasure her. In fact, the needy bitch thought something along the lines of *the more the merrier* when it came to these two particular tigers. It didn't want anyone else. Just these two. Singly, or as a pair, it didn't matter. It just wanted them both. Forever.

She took a deep breath and decided to just go for it. Why was she still hesitating? What was she worried about? Whatever happened next, the Mother of All seemed to have a hand in Jacki's fate. It was a leap of faith, but then, Jacki's recent life had been full of such leaps and the Goddess had never failed her yet. Jacki made up her mind. Finally.

"I *am* willing," she answered Geir's earlier question. "I'm sorry I've been so confused." She rose up on her elbows, looking at each of the men in turn.

"No more confused than the rest of us, I think." Beau leaned in to give her a kiss on the cheek that somehow fueled her inner fire. But he pulled back, sitting at her side, just looking at her. "You're beautiful, Jacki. And special. We'll do whatever you want—including forget this whole idea, if that's what you decide."

"For now, I want to see where this could lead," she said bravely, sitting up and reaching for both of them. She kissed Beau and then turned to kiss Geir, the quiet man at her side, watching her with such intensity that it almost stole her breath. "I have to believe the Mother of All led us to this for a reason. Even Bettina agrees and if you can't trust the word of the High Priestess, who can you trust, right?" She laughed a bit, but the moment was still tense. She could fix that. If she was brave enough.

Gathering her courage, Jacki let the sheet that had covered her slip down to her waist as she sat up fully. She brought Beau's hand to one of her breasts, Geir's to the other, inviting them to touch her.

They moved slowly at first, but the sensations were like nothing Jacki could have predicted. Two such different touches—but both were perfect. Geir, the quieter man, was downright combustible and touched her with a slightly rougher edge that made her tremble. But Beau's habitual anger completely calmed when he touched her and the gentle strokes of his fingers made her weak in the knees. She wondered how this would work but the moment she showed the slightest hesitation, Beau took control.

Beau ripped the covers off the bed, leaving Jacki in the center of the huge bed, crowded by the men on either side. Beau smiled as he worked his way over to nibble on her ear. He still had one hand on her breast and he squeezed gently as he claimed her lips.

Meanwhile, Geir was using his mouth on her other breast. He then moved downward, licking the underside and even taking a gentle bite at her skin that made her squeak with unexpected pleasure. She giggled against Beau's mouth as Geir continued gently nibbling his way down over her belly.

Beau broke the kiss and looked downward, as if gauging Geir's progress. Geir must have sensed his scrutiny because he lifted his head and even Jacki could see the question in his eyes. But Beau shrugged.

"You said you wanted a taste of her cream. Have at it, my friend," Beau said outrageously.

Geir grinned in a way that could only be called devilish before lowering his head once more. He moved his body around so that he was at her feet and then, as Beau's lips returned to hers, she felt Geir's hands part her knees. She was powerless to resist anything they wanted to do to her at this point—though to be honest, resistance was the farthest thing from her mind. She was reveling in the feeling of being the object of desire for these two amazing, virile, fierce men.

Between Beau kissing her senseless and Geir's demanding touches as he parted her knees and then prowled his way between her legs as if he had every right to just park himself in her most sensitive areas, she was lost. Completely lost to the amazing sensations these two men aroused in her body. Geir let her feel his hot breath against her inner thigh before he licked her there, following with a tender bite that made her squirm.

And then he licked her. Right *there*. His tongue rasped over her clit and she couldn't stifle the moan that rose to her lips. Beau drew back, letting her come up for air and she was able to concentrate on the feel of Geir's hands gripping her thighs, then moving around to spread her wide open for his inspection.

When he didn't do anything more for a moment, her curiosity made her lift her head so she might see what was going on. She gasped as she met Geir's gaze. He was lying on his stomach between her spread thighs, his fingers tracing patterns around her folds as he looked at her. His gaze met hers and she never would have believed blue eyes could get so hot. She saw the faint hint of a smile on his lips and in his eyes that warmed her from the depths of her soul.

This quiet man who didn't smile much was smiling now from the deepest, hidden parts of himself. She had brought that joy to him. Somehow, she had been able to give him that and it made her feel like a benevolent goddess. Jacki marveled for a moment. She had never once in her life felt like a sex goddess. She hadn't thought she had it in her. If she'd thought about it at all, she would have said she'd be destined for a very simple sex life—if she had much of one at all. She had never been terribly adventurous sexually, but it seemed like she was making up for lost time now. Heaven help her.

Geir held her gaze as he lowered his mouth, fastening his lips to the little nub in a way that made her want to scream in pleasure. Her breath came in short pants as her excitement grew. Geir's eyes promised so much more, encouraging her to let go as he sucked on her clit.

When he slid two thick fingers into her, she came hard against his mouth. She couldn't help herself. She had never had such an intense encounter before and it hit her hard. Geir rode her through the climax, but didn't let go. In fact, he began to thrust his fingers in a shallow rhythm that didn't let the fire inside her die. No, it fanned the flames higher as he nibbled on her most sensitive areas with gentle, yet firm touches.

"Now that was a thing of beauty," Beau commented, drawing her attention. "What do you say, Geir? One more time? Maybe we can get her to scream this time." Geir seemed to rise to Beau's challenge because suddenly his tongue was flicking against her clit in a way that was almost guaranteed to make her squirm. Beau lowered his head to her breasts, sucking and tugging gently with his teeth, pinching and stroking with his hands. Between the two men, four hands and two mouths tormenting her, Jacki came quickly once more, crying out as she spasmed in renewed ecstasy.

Beau lifted his head when her body quieted a bit, making a tsking sound and shaking his head. "You didn't scream." He sighed dramatically. "You know you've given us a challenge now, don't you?"

"I didn't mean to," she admitted, playing his game. It was a fun game, after all.

"I don't know," Beau pretended to think about her words. She felt Geir disengage, sitting up between her legs as he removed his fingers from inside her. "Do you think we need to try something else, Master Geir?" Beau asked, looking at the other man.

"Indeed I do," Geir managed to say, though it was pretty obvious he was highly aroused and very close to the edge. It must've been obvious to Beau too, because he moved back a bit and gestured politely toward Geir.

"I think she wants to be fucked now," Beau said outrageously. "What do you think?"

"I think if I don't get inside her in the next minute, I'll die," Geir answered rather dramatically.

But his urgency made a similar feeling rise inside Jacki as she watched the way his shoulder muscles couldn't quite contain a fine tremor of need.

"Come into me now, Geir," she whispered. "I need you too." Jacki spread her thighs as wide as they would go as Geir moved into position. He scooped both of his hands under her butt and simply lifted her hips to meet his while he knelt on the bed.

It was a different position than she'd ever been in before, but it was outrageously sexy. Geir used his massive strength, his arm and shoulder muscles bunching and flexing, glistening with a fine sheen of sweat while he brought her over himself, sheathing his hard cock inside her with slow, deliberate, unstoppable movements.

He was thick and hard and finally—finally—inside her. Where, her heart told her once and for all, he belonged.

CHAPTER EIGHT

Geir slid home and stopped. He stopped breathing. Stopped thinking. He just stopped for a moment out of time and felt the rightness of where he was and what he was doing.

He had experienced moments like this before, but never during a sexual situation. It was a moment to remember. To observe and collect. To hold against the ages. A moment of discovery. A moment of revelation.

Jacki Kinkaid was part of him now, as he was part of her. No matter what happened in the future, or what he had to sacrifice to keep her in his life, he would do it. He was her slave and her protector. Her lover and…if the Goddess willed it…her love.

Only time would tell. And with that thought, time started again. He began to move within her, feeling the way her tight walls squeezed him, caressing him, welcoming him. It was almost too much to bear.

His inner tiger rose in a way that it never had with other women. It was only with Jacki that Geir lost some of his legendary control. The Master was the pupil when it came to Jacki and what she did to him. She turned him inside out and upside down. He was just lucky she didn't seem to mind when his tiger got away from him.

It felt so good to finally make love to her. So right. So

perfect.

And then Beau moved, lifting Jacki's head so that she could rest in his lap, giving Geir a better angle. Oddly he didn't mind. His inner tiger was cooperating too. It saw Beau as a brother of sorts. A companion in the task of bringing their female pleasure. That was its focus. Pleasuring Jacki was all that mattered to the cat.

Geir was overwhelmed by his first taste of being inside Jacki, but he knew that even if he finished quickly, Beau would pick up the slack and it wouldn't be too long before Geir could try—and succeed—in pleasing her again. It felt good to have a partner in this task. Someone who could keep Jacki at a fever pitch while Geir got his act together.

It was a surety that he wasn't going to last long this first time. Then again, judging by the way her flesh quivered around him, Jacki wasn't going to last either. Not this time. They were both in synch when his pulses became short, almost violent digs, his body trembling in time with hers when he growled and came hard inside her.

Geir let her legs down gently, barely able to get air as he came down from a very high place. He had never felt such pleasure before and it was more than a little overwhelming. He took care with her body, stroking his hands over her quivering thighs as they closed of their own accord. He'd ridden her hard and in what he could tell was a position to which she was unaccustomed. He would have to make it up to her. She had been so accommodating, so willing to do anything he asked of her.

And his beast had demanded. It had goaded him into taking her hard and fast, the way it desired. The beast had been in control for a while there, and Geir was a little shocked by its desire to come into the forefront when it came to pleasing their woman. But Geir supposed he shouldn't have been too surprised. The tiger within him played a supporting role most of the time, letting the man rule over the body when it wasn't in cat form. Most shifters—Beau most notably—had to fight the beast for supremacy, even when wearing their human guise.

But Geir had always been different. Now though, since he had found Jacki, all bets were off. She tempted him like no other female and when he was with her, he lost all of his infamous control.

He lay down at her side, placing his head on her midsection. His cat purred when she ran her fingers through his hair in the aftermath of the greatest passion he had ever known.

"You are amazing, Jacki," he whispered, knowing she would hear him with her sharp shifter senses.

"You're not so bad yourself, Geir," she said in a slightly rough voice, a tone he had never heard from her before.

He lifted his head and realized that Beau hadn't moved. Beau couldn't help the struggle he fought every day with the tiger within. His anger was very close to the surface, but Geir had noted how calm Beau was when he was with Jacki. She soothed Beau's beast and let the man come to the fore. Just the opposite of what happened for Geir.

Geir moved, knowing that Beau needed her too. Somehow, he didn't mind. In fact, he sort of looked forward to watching Jacki take her pleasure with the other tiger—his new brother. There was a deep and true bonding going on here. It was much more profound than Geir would have guessed.

He knelt at her side, watching as Beau moved, taking the lead. Their eyes met over her body and Geir nodded at Beau's questioning look. Beau moved carefully around him, probably well aware that Geir's tiger had been in charge moments ago. There was no doubt that Beau knew to be careful of other shifters when the beast was in control.

Geir also felt a sense of pride that Beau was careful of his reaction in particular, because it meant that Beau saw him as an equal. A lesser tiger wouldn't have concerned Beau, who was a strong Alpha in his own right. The fact that Beau was wary meant he respected Geir's tiger, which made the cat preen a bit and feel even more benevolent toward the man-cat it now considered its brother.

That had happened fast. But such was the way with the animal sides of their nature. Frequently, the beast knew faster than the human what to make of any given situation. The beast had recognized its mate almost instantly. It had taken Geir's human side a little while to catch up. It seemed the same thing was happening with this threesome. The beasts didn't object and the human sides were beginning to come around.

Geir watched as Beau leaned over and kissed their woman, rolling a short distance away, taking her to her side as he faced her and brought her into his body. She went with a willing eagerness that made Geir oddly glad. They weren't pushing her into this. They weren't making her do anything she didn't want to do. She wanted this too. He could see it in every line of her needy body.

Geir reached out and stroked her spine as Beau lifted her leg, angling in to join his body to hers. Geir's breath caught as he watched Beau take possession of their woman. Their mate. And the fire in his gut began to churn anew. He'd never seen anything hotter in his entire life.

Geir lay down behind her, stroking her back, her curvy ass, her delicate arm…any area he could reach on her soft body, while Beau possessed her. Geir was content to watch and wait. The cat inside him knew something momentous was happening here. For once, it counseled him to wait. To stalk. To hunt the thing that was coming on the horizon. Geir didn't have a clue what the cat was talking about, but he had learned to listen to his instincts. He waited…and watched.

And damn if that didn't make him hard again.

Jacki made little noises as Beau pushed into her over and over, driving her higher and higher. When the wave broke, she cried out and Beau went stiff in her arms. Geir felt the bed shake with their reaction and it made him want her all over again. He wanted to feel that bliss. To experience that ultimate high.

And he could. He just had to wait a bit for her to be ready

again. He had a feeling she would accept him. She was his mate, after all.

And after what he'd just witnessed, there was no doubt in his mind that she was Beau's mate as well.

Beau pulled out after the spasms of ecstasy subsided, rolling to his back. Geir wound his hand around Jacki's middle, pulling her back against him. She seemed content to lie against him as she caught her breath.

After a while, he realized she would probably want to clean up. The bed too, would need a change if they wanted to sleep here tonight. No way was he letting her out of his arms—even for the few hours left until morning. He decided to take the lead while Beau was recovering.

He got up and lifted Jacki in his arms, heading for the biggest of the bathrooms on this level, which as luck would have it, was attached to Jacki's room. It was a shared bathroom between this room and the one next door, which was Geir's. They could clean up and then go use the king bed in his room. Geir didn't think Beau would object, and it made him pause only a moment to realize that he was including the other man in whatever came next.

As it should be, he thought. Their cats had found a way to coexist. Now it looked like their human sides would figure it out as well.

Geir put Jacki down when he reached the oversized shower. There was a teak wood bench along the back of the large stall. He placed her there, in a sitting position, while he adjusted the programmable shower to a warm setting.

"You take such good care of me," Jacki observed sleepily. She made a pretty picture, leaning to one side, resting her head against the marble tile along the wall.

"It'll be even better in a minute. I promise." He finished fussing with the water jets and sprayer heads and went over to help her stand. She was weary, but smiling as they stepped into the mist of warm water together.

"Oh, this is heaven," she sighed, leaning back against his chest as the water sluiced over them both. Her eyes closed for a moment before she straightened and reached out for the bottle of shower gel.

She squirted some into her hand and then offered it to him, squirting a dollop into his palm when he offered it. Instead of using it on himself, he rubbed his hands together, creating a foam which he then applied to her shoulders with long, tender strokes.

He worked his way down her arms when she stilled, seeming to soak in his caresses and massaging touch. He worked on her shoulders and neck for a moment before taking his hands down, over her soft breasts, pausing to cup and squeeze. The point of the shower was to get clean, but they could have a little fun while they were at it, couldn't they?

She moaned when he stroked lower, over her mons and down into her neatly trimmed curls. The way her slippery skin slid over his body heightened his pleasure as she squirmed against him. At this rate, he would take her again without the least bit of hesitation if she but asked.

"Is this a private party, or can anyone join in?" Beau's amused voice came to them from the other end of the steamy shower area.

Jacki straightened a bit, craning her neck to look at Beau. "Only specially invited guests," she quipped, apparently more awake than Geir had thought.

Maybe he would get a chance to have her again before they slept. He hadn't wanted to push her for more, but if she was awake and willing to play, all bets were off. His inner tiger growled in satisfaction.

"Oh. So am I invited?" Beau continued to tease as he stepped into the shower and moved closer.

"Consider yours a permanent invitation," Jacki answered as she reached over to snag Beau's hand and draw him near. She reached up to kiss him long and deep while Geir ran his still soapy hands over her body.

When she stepped back from Beau, she turned in Geir's arms and gave him the same, long, hot, sultry kiss. Geir's hands went to her wet hair and slid into the tangled depths, holding her mouth close while his tiger came to the fore. She didn't seem to mind, thank the Goddess, that his human side went out of control every time she kissed him.

What followed was a flurry of soapy sliding strokes from her hands, his hands, occasionally Geir collided with Beau's hands on a particularly luscious piece of Jacki's real estate, but it didn't matter. All that mattered in the moment of steamy, wet, slippery, sexy fun was that Jacki wanted them both and was eager to show them exactly how she wanted them and where. She wasn't shy about ordering them around, which was an intriguing change. Geir had never been with a woman who felt free to give the orders in the bedroom.

Of course, they weren't in the bedroom. They were in a steamy world where only the three of them existed. The three of them...and the passion that rose like a storm to bathe them in its fury. Jacki demanded and the men responded. She lifted up, showing Geir in no uncertain terms what she wanted and he gave it to her.

He slid into her, facing her, one of his hands positioned to hold her leg up at his side, his fingers under her knee. Much to his surprise, she stilled him when he would have begun to move. Watching, he was a little dumbfounded—and a whole lot excited—when she gestured to Beau to come up behind her.

"Come in back," she told Beau in a soft, whispery voice barely heard above the whooshing sound of the water.

"Are you serious?" Beau let his incredulity sound in his voice. Geir felt a mirroring kind of astonishment. Did she really mean what it sounded like?

"I've done it before. Not often, but a time or two. You won't hurt me," she assured Beau. Use the slippery stuff. It'll go in easier.

"Sweet Mother of All," Beau breathed as she pointed toward a bottle of bath oil sitting innocently on the shelf built into the tiled wall. "Are you sure?"

"Knock it off, Beau. Give me what I want!" Her

impatience seemed to decide Beau. He reached for the bottle of bath oil and squeezed out a generous portion into his hand. Geir couldn't see what he did next, but he certainly felt it when Beau made an appearance a very short distance from where Geir was already joined with her.

Jacki couldn't believe the feeling of having them both inside her. It she was being honest, this was the delicious fulfillment of a long-held fantasy that she figured would never come true. How wrong she'd been! And how lucky she was now, to be experiencing this—with these two incredibly special men.

She felt stretched beyond all comprehension, but somehow nothing hurt. Nothing was too much. All was right with her world. Finally. And forever.

She encouraged them to move, helpless, yet holding all the cards in this position, balanced between two strong Alphas. Just where she wanted to be.

Sweet Mother of All! Could she die of this kind of pleasure? If so, it would be worth it. Oh, so worth it.

Geir seemed reluctant to move at first, but then his tiger growled—a sexier sound she had never heard—and took over. She would have to kiss his furry nose the next time she saw him wearing his stripes. His beast half had saved this situation from stalling out before it even got going.

What happened next was a bit of a blur of straining and stroking, moving and trembling on the precipice of a pleasure she had never known. When she finally went over the edge, she realized almost at once her men came with her.

At the exact moment of completion, another very potent wave of magic spread over them all as the mating bond snapped into place like a taut rubber band. Jacki was glad the guys were holding her up because she had never felt anything like it. The strength of the bond stole her breath.

The men slipped from her body and seemed to be almost as surprised and weakened by the bond's formation as she was. Geir took her with him as he all but collapsed on the bench at the rear of the spacious shower stall. She ended up on his lap with Beau slouched against the wall on her other side. There was just enough room for both of the guys on the teak bench, even though it made some alarming creaking noises with all three of them on it.

But none of them cared. The whole house could collapse at that moment and Jacki realized they wouldn't care.

"Whoa," Beau vocalized the weary surprise they were all feeling. "What was that?"

"Mating bond." Jacki caught her breath as she leaned half on Geir and half on the cold tile of the wall behind her. "I think."

"What else could it have been?" Geir asked, hugging her closer for just a moment. "It was the Mother Goddess's benediction on our union. Our triple union. No going back on it now, I guess."

"Would you want to?" Jacki asked, frowning when she heard the plaintive note in her voice.

Geir bent down to kiss her forehead. "Never in a million years. You are mine now, Jacki. For now and for always."

Beau lifted her foot playfully and nibbled on her big toe before kissing the sole of her foot.

"You're ours now, kitten. No getting out of it. Ever," Beau promised playfully, even while emphasizing the fact that she belonged to both of them. Just as she wanted it.

"Does this mean we can do that again anytime we want?" she asked with a fond little smile. She wanted more. A whole lot more.

"Most definitely," Beau replied without hesitation. "I think I can speak for both of us when I say we are at your disposal singly or as a pair, anytime, anyplace, any way you want us. Right, G?"

Geir nodded solemnly. "Most definitely," he agreed, then smiled softly. "I didn't expect the bond to affect us like that. You felt it too, right?"

"Yeah, I felt it. Like a wave of magic hitting me in the face and filling my being with the…rightness, I guess you'd call it," she agreed. "It was momentous." She wasn't sure it happened to all shifters like it had happened to them, but then again, this triple mating was special in many ways. Why should this be any different?

"You can say that again," Beau said as he stood, clearly beginning to regain some of his equilibrium. "Let's rinse off and find a bed. I think we all might need to sleep off the magical whammy a bit. What do you say?"

"Sounds like a plan," she replied with a grin.

Beau held out one hand to her, which she took. He lifted her to her feet and back into the spray of the water. Geir followed close behind. This time they stuck to the task of getting clean, their bodies happily sated for the moment, though it was clear it wouldn't take much to ignite the fire of passion once more.

After they dried off, Geir led them into his bedroom and the fresh king-sized bed in there. Jacki crawled into the middle of the big expanse and claimed a pillow for herself before falling promptly asleep.

When they woke a few hours later, Jacki noticed something she hadn't quite registered before. Her personal magical level seemed to have gained a bit of oomph since last night. She would have to ask Bettina to be certain, but Jacki supposed this was another benefit of having mated with two very strong Alphas. Maybe it would dissipate in time, but for now it was a pretty heady feeling to have all this energy at her disposal.

While she would have liked to laze around in bed for a bit longer, there were many things to do today. First, she had to check on Tom and see if the spell they had worked last night had brought him out of his unconscious state. Bettina had said that it could take time to see the full effect of the magic-working they had done last night.

"Come on guys!" She slapped two perfect, muscled butts—one on either side of her. Damn, her mates were pretty. "Up and at 'em!" She tried to wake them up, but neither seemed to want to move. "What? Did I wear you out, kitties?" she said in a sing-song teasing voice.

"Stop being so cheerful," Beau groused from her left. "It's too early to be up yet."

"No it isn't. It's well past sunrise and we've got places to go and people to see today. Rise and shine sleepy tigers!" She tried to coax them into moving, but neither one seemed to want to lift their heads from the pillows.

"This is technically our honeymoon, Jacki," Geir mumbled half into his pillow on her right. "Give a guy a break and let us sleep just a little more."

At that point, Jacki realized the guys weren't handling the magical shift in their energies as well as she was, and she grew concerned. She climbed out of the bed, crawling out at the foot of the giant bed, between the two slumbering giants. She had to talk to Bettina before she really started to worry about her new mates. Maybe this was normal? Or maybe she had real reason to worry.

"Okay guys. You two sleep a little bit more. I'm going to check on things. I'll be back in a few minutes." She tiptoed out of Geir's room through the attached bath and into her own room, grabbing some clothes and dressing hastily. Almost as an afterthought, she stripped the sheets off the bed as she went, taking them with her to dump in the washing machine she'd seen in the utility room down the hall.

She had checked on Tom, saddened to see him still unconscious, but heartened by the fact that his color was much better. He hadn't taken a turn for the worse in the night. If anything, he appeared to be stabilizing.

Tad and Mandy had taken turns with Bettina watching him through the night and all reports were much more positive than they had been to this point. Tom had improved significantly since they had performed the spell the night before. Jacki left him in Mandy's capable hands and was directed toward the kitchen where she was told, Bettina was awaiting her arrival. Which was perfect, because Jacki really needed to talk to the High Priestess.

"Is it normal for them to be so wiped out while I'm so…energetic?" Jacki asked Bettina a few minutes later as they sat at the kitchen table drinking coffee. Bettina had assured her quickly that nothing was wrong with her mates— after giving her a congratulatory hug for her newly mated status.

"The three of you are joined now on several levels," Bettina explained. "The physical is the least of them. You are also joined on a spiritual plane, and a magical one. It will take some time before the new levels of your shared magic settle. From what you've said, it seems like maybe your mates were giving last night, during the joining of your hearts and souls. You were on the receiving end, so to speak, right?"

Jacki tried not to blush as she nodded.

"Don't worry." Bettina reached across the table to put her hand over the top of Jacki's. "Many women will be envious of your arrangement. You'll get used to it in time. If you need pointers on how to deal with it, you should talk to Allie."

"Mate of the Lords?" Jacki was nonplussed. She might be familiar with the king of all lion shifters because he was kin, but she had never mixed in such exalted company on a regular basis. The idea of just calling the priestess Allesandra up as if she were an old friend was a little intimidating.

"You're going to have to get used to dealing with all levels of shifter society, Jacki. I minister to the least among them and the greatest. If you are my apprentice, so will you."

"It's all a lot to get used to," Jacki hedged.

"And yet Sam Kinkaid speaks highly of you," Bettina observed rather than ask a question. Jacki knew the question was implied.

"Sam is kin. He's more like a pesky older brother than a king." Jacki laughed at her own description. "Okay. Maybe that's just how he is to me because I know him so well. He definitely can roar with the best of them."

"So I've heard," Bettina agreed with a smile. "What do you think of Ria and Jake?"

"Nice people. Ria's kind of amazing and Jake's a total badass." Jacki giggled as she said it, hearing the pitter-patter—okay, the stomp and glide—of Beau and Geir coming into the kitchen.

"Who's a badass?" Geir asked.

At the same time Beau said, "Talking about me again, sweets?"

Jacki stood, relief flooding her that they looked okay. Both were dressed and though Beau was yawning, neither of them had the dark circles under their eyes that she'd feared. She rushed to them, giving each a hug and a peck on the cheek. She couldn't control her smile of relief.

CHAPTER NINE

"So who's the badass?" Geir repeated as he pulled out her chair for her.

"And why are you looking at anyone's ass but mine?" Beau teased, goosing her butt playfully as she sat down.

"I was talking about Jake. He seems like a badass for a human. That's all. I wasn't commenting on his actual ass, though I have noticed that's also rather fine in an objective sort of way." She teased them right back as Bettina laughed her tinkling laughter that invited everyone who heard it to join in.

"No more noticing anyone's butt but ours," Beau shook a spatula at her as he took up a position in front of the stove. Geir was raiding the fridge, tossing out ingredients to Beau as if they'd done this a thousand times before. Apparently the men were going to make eggs and bacon for breakfast. "But I'll give you a pass this time..." Beau added, "...because you couldn't have seen him since we mated. So the assessment had to have been made before we hooked up. Now that we're official though, we'll have no more of that, if you please."

He tried to sound stern, but failed, although he didn't seem to care. He turned back to his stove, breaking eggs into a frying pan and turning into a short order cook before her eyes, while Geir went to work making a small mountain of toast. Her men appeared to have hidden talents.

Jacki marveled at the way Beau had changed in such a short time. The tiger who was angry all the time and never far beneath his human surface, had become a pussy cat nearly overnight. It was amazing what a little thing like a mating could do for a bad-tempered kitty.

They were well into breakfast when there was a tap at the back door to the kitchen. Geir opened it to admit Ria, Jake, and a small contingent of their Royal Guards. Unfortunately, neither Ria nor Jake looked like this was a purely social call.

Geir invited them all to sit in the giant, family kitchen and everyone soon found seats and cups of coffee. A few took advantage of the leftover toast or bacon, grabbing a quick nibble while they got down to business.

"All the teams have reported in and although we didn't find any more cameras, we did find evidence of that same vehicle stopping at different points around the property. The guy has been prowling our perimeter for at least the past few days," Jake reported, all business now.

"We also found two instances of tigers being filmed on the cameras you found. There could be more, but the techs are pretty confident that we recovered at least ninety percent of the old data that was set to be recorded over," Ria added.

"Damn," Beau commented, the angry tiger coming to the fore now that other people were around. Jacki reached over and placed her hand on his, feeling him calm a bit at her touch.

"So the watcher now knows there are tigers here, if he didn't before," Geir stated. "And now he has proof."

"That's about the size of it," Jake confirmed.

"So what's the plan?" Beau asked, impatience clear in his tone, though he seemed to be holding his usual anger at bay for now.

"I think we need to go hunting," Geir said in a low, deadly voice. Jacki felt a quiver in her tummy at the look in his eye when she realize this lethal warrior was her mate. She looked at Beau's determined face and felt the same little quiver. He looked just as fierce.

"If we do this right, he'll come to us," Jake said softly, drawing all eyes.

It was pretty well known by now that Jake was a seer. He had foreseen things that had helped win the last big battle against the *Venifucus* in North Carolina. Although he couldn't shapeshift, he had the respect of every person in the room. Hands down.

"What do you recommend?" Geir asked, his head tilted as if in respectful consideration.

"We should set traps where the tall pines converge near a rocky meadow. We'll catch him there, and if we play it all very carefully, we might be able to work this to our advantage. Exactly how, I can't say yet. It might come clearer, or it might not. All I know is, we need to handle this guy very carefully."

"Right now, he only knows about tigers, so I suggest we limit the people he deals with to the tigers among us," Ria said. Jacki felt a little pang of dread. She looked at her mates.

Geir and Beau had a gleam of satisfaction in their eyes when they heard Ria's words, but Jacki worried. Her new mates and the Millers were the only tigers left on the mountain. The Millers had a small cub, so they shouldn't be asked to deal with an individual that could be potentially dangerous to their child. And cubs needed their parents. Neither Beau nor Geir would ask the Millers to knowingly walk into danger at this point.

Jacki listened as the warriors planned out the traps they would lay, and organized coverage to check them around the clock. It was decided that the Royal Guards could help watch, but when it came to confronting the watcher, Geir and Beau would take point. They would have to be on call at all times until the trap was sprung.

Bettina surprised her by volunteering herself and Jacki to set the traps. Apparently these were going to be magical traps, not just conventional man traps. Jacki wasn't really sure what help she would be with something like that, but it was yet another unexpected thing she would have to learn if she was going to be Bettina's backup.

As the impromptu meeting drew to a close, the Royal Guards filed out first to run a search of the area and check with those who had been left stationed outside. Only after the Guard was confident that there were no hidden dangers outside the house would Ria and Jake be permitted to leave.

Jake seemed impatient with the procedure, but willing to humor the Guard—at least for a little while. Jacki secretly wondered how long it would be before the human warrior would get completely fed up with the precautions and strike out on his own. Jacki gave him another few weeks before the first big confrontation, but she didn't tell anyone her thoughts. Not yet. She might share her observation with her mates later, but that's as daring as she would get speculating about the *pantera noir* royals.

Ria, more comfortable with the precautions for her safety, used the time to speak with Jacki somewhat privately. She stood near the coffee pot where Jacki was pouring another cup for herself and her mates.

"We didn't bother you with all this last night because Bettina told us she needed all three of you to help Tom," Ria said. "I volunteered to help too, but Bettina said my power would be counterproductive. Something to do with the moon…" she trailed off, but Jacki thought she understood.

"We called on the Light represented by the light of the moon. Which is why we had to wait until the moon rose last night to do the spell," Jacki answered the unspoken question. "Your power is of the new moon—when the face of the moon is dark and the veil between worlds is weakest."

Ria seemed to take in the information with interest. "So it's true then that you're going to be Bettina's apprentice?"

Jacki wasn't sure how to answer. Then again, this was the Nyx—the queen of the small, but mighty *pantera noir* Clan. Jacki had to be honest with her.

"That appears to be the plan, milady."

"Call me Ria. And congratulations on your mating. Jake was a little scandalized when he foresaw you with both Geir and Beau, but I say more power to you. Although I wouldn't trade Jake for anything in the world, I'm a little envious. Just don't tell Jake I said that." Ria's engaging laugh invited Jacki to join her mirth.

Somehow the Nyx's words and easy acceptance made Jacki feel better. If others felt the same, then maybe Jacki's worries would turn out to be unfounded. If not, well, they would deal with that as it happened. No way was she giving up her mates. They were hers now and no small-minded attitudes from anyone would tear them apart.

Jake came over and put his arm around Ria, kissing the top of her head. "We're ready to go now," he told his mate. Jacki could see the glow of happiness around them, despite all the challenges they had faced—and would face—as a couple.

Being the monarch of an entire race of shifters wasn't easy. And being the target of evil was certainly no picnic. But they had weathered the storm and come out the other side. For now.

"Congratulations," Jake said to Jacki. "I hope you'll be very happy."

Jacki couldn't help but smile. It was clear the human seer was more than a little confused by the threesome, but he seemed willing to go with the flow. Jacki felt her respect for the man, which had already been high, grow even further.

"Thank you," Jacki responded simply.

A Royal Guard came over and ushered the royal pair out through the kitchen door. The kitchen was empty except for Jacki and her mates, and Bettina.

"Well," Bettina said, standing and putting her empty coffee mug in the dishwasher. "It appears we have a great deal of work to do this morning." She looked directly at Jacki.

"We do?" Jacki had thought the plan was to set the magical traps that afternoon. Had she missed something?

"You bet we do," Bettina answered brightly. "It takes preparation to set the kinds of traps they were talking about. And you, my dear, are a babe in the woods. A fish on dry land. Out of your depth, so to speak." Bettina chuckled at her own analogies. "I've got to show you a few things before we attempt the work they want us to do later today. There's no time to waste."

So much for a relaxing morning spent with her mates, Jacki thought morosely.

"It's okay," Beau came over to Jacki and hugged her with one arm around her shoulders. "We have a lot to prepare as well. Securing our home territory—and our mate—has to be our top priority." He kissed her and let her go.

"The guy who's watching the border isn't after me, silly. He's probably after the Nyx," she reminded him.

Beau frowned. "Either situation is totally unacceptable."

Geir grinned and stepped forward to give Jacki a quick hug and kiss. "Watch it, Beau, you almost sounded like a Royal Guard there for a moment."

Beau paused with one hand on the doorknob of the kitchen door. He looked thoughtful. "I did, didn't I?"

Geir clapped him on the back, joining him by the door. "We'll make a respectable warrior out of you yet, my friend. I think your mercenary days are over."

"Truth be told, they were over the minute I laid eyes on Jacki," Beau admitted. Jacki felt a little rush at his words but there was no time to pursue that feeling. They all had work to do.

The men left to go do whatever they needed to do in way of preparations and Jacki spent the rest of the morning with Bettina, learning all sorts of things she had never expected. The ways of magic were both complex and beautifully simple. It really was an honor to learn these things from a master of the craft. Hours passed in the blink of an eye and before she knew it, they were making lunch in the big kitchen.

They all dined together, plus a few of the Royal Guards who had been helping Geir and Beau make preparations. There wasn't a chance for any deep conversation with all the other people around, but Jacki just enjoyed being in her mates' presence. She felt better when they were around—more complete.

After lunch, they all trooped out to the woods together and began the real work of laying the traps—both magical and mundane.

"Tom's spirit still dwells in darkness," Bettina said later that night after they'd had dinner.

Tad and Mandy had again stayed close to the house, looking after their cub and Tom during the day. Now it was just the four of them—Bettina, Jacki, Geir and Beau—gathered in Tom's bedroom, looking after him and plotting their next move. Or rather, Bettina was plotting. She led the group, since magic was her specialty.

Beau didn't know how old the High Priestess was, but she had been High Priestess for as long as anyone he knew remembered, which was quite a long time indeed. She'd had decades, if not centuries, to perfect her skills.

Rumor had it Bettina was at least part fey, so it was very possible she'd been around that long. Shifters were long-lived, but fey…well, they were the next best thing to immortal. Or so the stories said.

"So how do we bring him back to the Light?" Jacki asked, worry clear on her pretty face. She was very anxious about her brother and Beau would do anything he could to help take that worry away.

"We've made good progress the last two times we tried to intervene, cutting off the source that was draining him and beginning to reverse some of the damage," Bettina reminded them. "Tonight we'll try to do even more. I propose a change in tactics. We've been coming at this from a healer's perspective. Tonight, we must adopt the attitude of a warrior. We're going on the offensive."

"How are we going to do that?" Beau wanted to know.

It all sounded very strange to him, even though he'd grown up with a magical, priestess mother. He was coming to understand that the High Priestess—and her new apprentice—were practicing the magical arts on a whole other level.

Bettina smiled at him. "Jacki and I have been working on exactly that today. And actually, you're going to play a very large role in the night's activities. We need your anger, Beau Champlain." Bettina turned to look at Geir. "And we need your cunning, Master Geir. The two together will help us prevail. I feel sure of it."

"But we're not mages. We don't know how to do spells," Geir protested, voicing Beau's objections as well.

"You forget. You are joined on a soul-level with Jacki now. She is the one who will draw the magic and allow you to see what is happening. You only need to direct her in how best to deploy our magical forces, if you will, Master Geir. And your bloodthirsty anger, Beau, will fuel the flames and expand the energy into a fireball of intensity. At least, that's my hope." Bettina shrugged, but kept smiling. "I believe it will work. Jacki knows the way of it now. We will let her guide the work."

She held out her hands, taking one of Beau's and one of Geir's, motioning for them to join hands with Jacki. They formed a circle over Tom's bed, two on either side.

Jacki took a deep breath as Beau watched her. She had a determined look on her face. He wanted to help her, but didn't quite understand what he was supposed to do here, and then it happened.

Jacki spoke some words Beau didn't recognize, but he felt the power in them. They were magic words. Spell words. And suddenly the room disappeared and the only thing that remained was Tom, in the bed, within their circle. Beau was fascinated for a moment by the pure white glow of the circle formed by their joined hands and the way the glow extended out to encompass all of Tom, head to toe. Then he looked at Tom and realized Jacki's brother emanated a sickly, dark red color. An evil color that just looked wrong.

The tiger within Beau roared, sensing an enemy and Beau's human side recoiled, then wanted to go on the attack. Bettina had pegged it right. Beau's infamous anger rose at what had been done to harm Tom. Beau knew the other man as a decent guy, a brave warrior and a good brother to Jacki. Tom was lighthearted and pure of purpose. He didn't deserve this...red...evil...miasma that surrounded him. It made Beau sick with fury.

And then he felt Jacki's hand in his, siphoning off his anger, taking the energy of it and using it to battle the red cloud that surrounded Tom, beating it back with her words and her continued chanting. Beau looked at Geir and saw the other man's eyes narrowed in concern...and calculation. Beau could almost see the energy flowing from Geir to Jacki through their joined hands as she kept speaking words of high magic Beau had never heard before and probably wouldn't be able to remember if he tried. Such was the way of magical words, or so his mother had taught him.

Beau had never been able to see magic before and he figured it had something to do with the mating bond. Being mated to a future High Priestess was going to be interesting if this was the sort of thing he could expect from the future.

Jacki gripped his hand harder as her voice rose in volume and he concentrated on the red cloud around her brother. Was it weakening? Yes. It looked like it was thinning before the onslaught of her magic. But then it rebounded and Beau felt a surge of adrenaline in his body as the bestial anger that was never far from his surface came to the fore. He felt Jacki using his energy and he welcomed it. He wanted that red cloud gone.

Geir tugged on Jacki's hand, Beau saw, almost as if he were gesturing toward Tom's left shoulder. And then Beau saw it too—the concentrated attack on Tom's heart. That's where the poison had taken hold and what it targeted. Beau felt and saw Jacki redirect her attack. She fought for her brother's heart and little by little, it looked like she was winning.

Beau lost all sense of time and space. For this interlude, nothing existed but the four of them holding hands and Tom—and the evil thing that held him in its grip. Bettina was silent for the most part except when she occasionally added her magical tone to the chant Jacki kept repeating, changing words and intonation occasionally to battle the red fog that was slowly giving up its hold on Tom. They were winning, but it was an arduous battle.

Beau fed Jacki his anger and his energy. He knew Geir was doing the same—only with less anger. The Master was tightly wound and in control of his human form for the most part. Only in passion did Geir's tiger take over, Beau had learned, much to his surprise. He wasn't sure he was totally comfortable knowing such things about another man just yet, but he figured comfort would come in time. Jacki was worth any adjustment he would have to make in his thinking and his life.

He kept his focus on Tom, even as he felt his energy start to stutter. Anger helped him overcome the momentary weakness as he redoubled his efforts to give all he could to his mate so that she could direct their combined power.

It was worth every effort when Beau finally saw the red recede completely. Jacki had won the battle for her brother's heart. He was free of the sickly, blood-red taint when Jacki drew her chant to a close and pulled back her power. Beau's vision changed as the spell dissipated. He could no longer see the powerful ring of white light formed around their joined hands, but now that he knew it was there, he could almost feel it. He had learned a great deal more about magic tonight, and about his new mate's potential to wield it.

If Jacki could do battle with the horror that had squeezed her brother in its evil grip after only a day of tutoring, then given time, she would be a formidable High Priestess. Beau was weary but pleased with that thought when the spell ended. He swayed on his feet and saw Geir do the same, but Jacki looked a little better and Bettina seemed unaffected. Beau was certain Bettina had been fully participating in the sharing of energy—he had felt it through their joined hands—but she seemed to have an almost endless supply of that pure, white, healing magic at her disposal.

She gave him a little jolt of it before she let go of his hand

and he felt better. He suspected she did the same for Geir, since they both nodded at her in thanks at about the same time. She smiled at them and bent to check on Tom.

"He is much better, though still weak," she reported. "I'll stay with him. You three should get some sleep. You probably don't realize it, but it's after three a.m."

Beau was a little shocked. They had started their work around nine o'clock at night. If Bettina was right—and Beau had no reason to believe she would mislead them regarding the time—they had been standing here for six hours or more. Maybe time worked differently inside the magic circle they had formed. Or maybe his perception of the passage of time had changed because they had been so focused on helping Tom.

Either way, physically, it made sense. Beau ran a hand through his hair and realized he was exhausted. Bone weary. Ready to get horizontal and stay that way for several hours at least. Geir looked just as tired and Jacki only marginally less so.

"Tommy looks a lot better," Jacki said, running her fingers over her brother's hand.

Jacki bent to kiss Tom's cheek, combing his hair with her fingers. It was clear she loved her sibling very much, but she was also really tired. When she straightened, Beau reached for her, encouraging her to lean on him.

"You have turned the tide," Bettina confirmed. "I will watch over him to make sure it stays that way, but I think the three of you, working together, were enough to chase the worst of the darkness away."

"What was that red stuff?" Beau asked, wondering. He'd never seen anything like it before.

Bettina smiled at him, cocking her head. "Your connection is even stronger than I thought if you were able to perceive the taint. Did you see it too, Master Geir?"

Geir nodded. "I have never seen the like," he admitted. "I've never been able to perceive magic before. I assume that's what it was, right?"

Bettina clapped her hands together with clear satisfaction. "Exactly right. You were seeing it through your mate's eyes. Sharing her power as she connected with you to direct yours. This is wonderful. You three are working very well together already. It will be exciting to see how your powers evolve. But for now..." she looked back at Tom, "...I believe you have saved his life."

Jacki sobbed—just once—and Beau tightened his arm around her. She was crying, but it was with relief. Fatigue probably had something to do with her emotional outburst as well, but Beau didn't mind. She had done something amazing here tonight and saved her brother as a result. She was entitled to her moment. She'd been strong for so long—leading them through hours and hours of hard, magical work—and she never once complained or backed down. Now though, when all was secure and her brother was out of the woods, she deserved a bit of relief, and all the emotional support he could give her.

Bettina looked at Jacki with kind eyes. "You three should go get some sleep. Tom will be okay for now. The evil has been battled back and tomorrow we will do one last spell to bring him all the way home. For the moment, he is safe and you are exhausted. Go rest."

Jacki nodded at her mentor and Beau helped her out of the room, Geir preceding them to open the doors along their path. All plans for seduction and passion went flying out the same window that had taken almost all his strength. There would be no repeat of the pleasure they had shared tonight, but Beau couldn't work up the energy to do more than have a tiny moment of regret. He was still with Jacki, and they would rest together. That was enough for now.

They landed in Jacki's room, which was closest. Thank goodness all the guest rooms had king sized beds. Beau didn't get much farther than the bed before his strength gave out. He helped Jacki into the center, then promptly collapsed on one side, while Geir did the same on the other. That was the last he knew for several hours.

CHAPTER TEN

Geir felt really hung-over when he woke the next morning. The bedside clock said he'd only had, at most, four hours of sleep, but it was clear Jacki and Beau had had even less. They were nowhere to be seen and Geir suspected, from the scent of cooking bacon wafting down the hallway, they were most likely in the kitchen.

Geir went over yesterday's events in his mind as he rousted himself out of Jacki's bed and headed for the bathroom. He realized there was much to be done today and no time to lose. He moved through his morning routine on autopilot while he thought about how best to juggle everything he had on his list for the day.

But first, breakfast.

It wasn't as awkward as Geir had half-expected it to be, thanks mostly to the presence of the High Priestess and Beau's surprisingly joyful mood. He made jokes through the meal, causing them all to laugh at his nonsensical humor. It was such a change from his normal angry and gruff demeanor, it was refreshing to see. Jacki had wrought that change in Beau. Geir wondered what kind of changes she would make in him as well…if he stayed in this threesome.

It still didn't feel exactly right to his human sensibilities to be in three-way. It wasn't what he'd been raised to expect. It wasn't necessarily anything he had ever thought about. And although he felt the mating bond deep in his soul, he wondered if the other two wouldn't be better off without him weighing them down.

It was quite clear that Jacki had affected Beau for the better. But what had she brought out in Geir? So far, she'd only spiked his animal side into gaining control over his human form—something Geir had worked to avoid most of his adult life. His training was all about control, and she made him lose it.

Try as he might, he couldn't figure out how that was a good thing.

They had barely finished breakfast when duty called in the form of Bronson, one of the young Royal Guards, knocking on the kitchen door. Beau got up to answer it and it was pretty clear from the look on Bronson's face that something was up.

"We caught the guy," Bronson announced as he entered the kitchen. "He walked into a trap on the perimeter by Tad and Mandy's place. They're bringing him here. Tad says there's a room in the barn that has been reinforced to hold prisoners."

That was news to Geir, but then, there were a lot of nooks and crannies in his new home that he had yet to discover. Tad's quick tours could only cover so much each time they did one.

"Looks like our plans for the day have changed," Beau said, leaning back in his chair and stretching. Geir could see he was keyed up despite the casual pose.

"Jake wants Master Geir and the priestesses to be on hand, if you wouldn't mind," Bronson asked somewhat bashfully, looking at Bettina with a flush on his cheeks.

"That means you get all of us, son," Beau stated, standing up, his posture brooking no argument. "No way am I letting you have all the fun, G. Plus, someone needs to watch over the safety of the women while you're all busy with the tango."

"He's not a terrorist, Beau," Geir said with good-natured

humor as he too rose and started putting dishes in the sink.

"Might as well be," Beau grumbled. "I'll get my gear. Don't go anywhere without me." Beau gave the ladies a stern look before he took off down the hallway at double time.

They arrived at the dojo a short while later. Geir didn't like exposing Jacki to the enemy, but if there was no other way, he would watch over her. First though, he hoped to talk with the prisoner himself and find a way to limit the ladies' involvement.

Jake met them in the main room of the dojo. A contingent of Royal Guards was arrayed around the building and Jake seemed troubled. Even though he could see the future, he was still human. Geir had come to trust the man, but it was hard to gauge what his expression meant.

"I have to make a call. First though, I want the ladies to take a look at him through the glass," Jake said. "It's mirrored, so barring some kind of arcane magic, he won't see them. But I have to be sure of the guy's allegiances before we decide on our next moves here."

"What aren't you saying?" Beau asked, his voice laced with an angry growl.

Jake grimaced. "I think the guy is *Altor Custodis*. If that's the case, we need to figure out if he's working for one of the corrupt branches of the AC or merely a watcher."

"Either way, he can't be allowed to continue his surveillance activities," Geir said firmly before Beau could let his anger loose.

"You'll get no argument on that from me," Jake was quick to affirm. "But if he's innocent, we need to handle this differently than we will if he's corrupt. The *Altor Custodis* has been nothing but an observational organization until recently."

"That may be," Bettina spoke up. "But we now know the corruption in the *Altor Custodis* goes all the way to the top." Everyone was silent as the High Priestess spoke. "While the organization's goals have never been violent or evil before, that has changed. We will have to be very certain of this man's allegiances before we make any decisions."

"Agreed," Jake said, pulling out his phone. "I plan to call Ben Steel in on this. He knows the AC better than any of us and last I heard, he was still in North Carolina. He can get up here fast if I ask him."

"Let me get a look at him first," Bettina said, already on the move.

She glided rather than walked, Geir thought, moving faster than could keep up with as she went unerringly to the viewing room he'd only just discovered was part of his new domain.

They all followed her into the small room that was equipped with the promised two way glass. They could see the man on the other side, handcuffed to a conveniently placed pipe in one corner of the room.

"The *Altor Custodis*..." Bettina began speaking as if giving a lecture as Jacki reached her side. "Their brotherhood began around the same time as the *Venifucus*, but with much less evil purpose. Where the *Venifucus* were interested only in supporting their liege, Elspeth, the Destroyer of Worlds, the *Altor Custodis* formed when the humans of that long ago time became aware of Others in their midst. They were tasked by their leaders to watch and report on all supernatural creatures they knew about and to do their best to discover as many Others as they could. Their records of our bloodlines now go back many centuries and they still have agents all over the world, reporting back through their leadership structure."

"They track us all?" Beau asked, his anger still ramped up but under control from what Geir could see.

"As many of us as they are aware of," Bettina replied without looking at him. She was focusing her regard on the prisoner. "Many of their operatives are marked in some way. See the tattoo on his left forearm?" Bettina looked over at Jacki, as if waiting for her response. When Jacki nodded, Bettina continued. "That seems to be just a mundane tattoo. The mark of a soldier in the AC's employ. I don't sense any other marks on him. I would be able to see the glow of a magical tattoo, even through his clothing. The *Venifucus* marks their operatives with the magical tattoo so they can track their people willing or not. So far, so good with this guy..." Bettina trailed off as she continued to look at the prisoner.

After about three minutes more of intense scrutiny and a few mumbled words of high magic, she sighed and stepped away from the glass. She turned to Jake and nodded toward the phone still in his hand.

"Call Ben Steel. He might be able to help us sort this out in a way that could work to our advantage." Her pretty blue eyes narrowed shrewdly before she turned back to the window, taking Jacki's hand and talking to her pupil softly, giving instruction.

An hour later, Bettina had shared all sorts of information with Jacki about how to spot magical tattoos with the aid of a particular magic word they had found that worked with Jacki's brand of magic. She was seeing things in new ways that really amazed her if she took a moment to think about it. She had always had a lot of magic at her disposal, but with Bettina to show her how to tap into it in very specific ways, she was able to harness more of it than she ever had before.

There was no doubt that she was a changed woman from the one who had entered a battle not of her making in North Carolina those weeks ago. Since that showdown at the stream where she had called on the Lady's power and been answered beyond her wildest dreams, she had changed on a fundamental level that she was only just coming to understand. It might take years to fully grasp all the changes that had been made to her being in that split second of the Goddess's intervention, but it was a journey Jacki was willing—no, eager—to take.

For having touched the pure Light of the Goddess in her hour of greatest need, Jacki now knew the path her life was meant to take. Bettina might have taken her by surprise with the request to teach her how to be a priestess, but now that Jacki had had some time to assimilate at least some of what had happened, she saw very clearly that destiny was at work in her life, in surprising, gratifying, purely benevolent ways. At least for now.

She would follow where the path led her, with Bettina's guidance.

The guys had gotten coffee and snacks from somewhere and when Bettina finally ended their minute study of the man behind the glass, Jacki was surprised to find an hour had passed. She welcomed the cup of coffee Beau pressed into her hands and noticed Geir, acting chivalrous, doing the same for Bettina.

A warm wave of caring swept over her for both men. They had watched over her even when she was zoned out, listening to Bettina's lecture on how to evaluate a potential enemy from twenty feet away. She realized only then that her inner beast, which was always alert to danger, had felt safe with the two tiger males watching over her. It had stayed calm and allowed Jacki to give her full concentration to Bettina's lesson.

From the way Bettina grinned at her over the rim of her coffee cup, the High Priestess knew it too.

"Ben Steel is on his way up the mountain," Jake said as he walked back into the room. He had left earlier and hadn't been seen for at least an hour.

"How did he get here so fast?" Beau asked.

"He was already on his way," Jake said, smiling. He then shifted his gaze directly to Jacki, still grinning. "Seems your Aunt Sophia, called the fox Alpha and told him to send the human our way two days ago. They drove up from North Carolina with the express instructions to arrive today. I have to confess, I didn't see a thing about any of this." Jake sat down at the rectangular table on the side of the room around which they'd all gathered.

"There, there," Bettina reached out to pat Jake's hand. "Remember, you're newly mated. I suspect your seer's gift was giving you a bit of a holiday so you could spend time with your new mate and help begin to make this place into a nest of your own. Sophia Grantham was there to pick up the slack for you this time. Not every seer sees the same things, as you well know. You might have been too close to this to perceive it."

"Yeah, my ego is a little stung, but I'll get over it," Jake said easily. "I'm just glad he's almost here. I want to sort this out as soon as possible. Did you discover anything else?"

"From everything we can see from this distance, he looks like a normal human male. He has an obvious *Altor Custodis* connection, but nothing magical about him that I can detect from here," Bettina reported. "Jacki and I tried several different magical methods to coax hidden things into view and they produced no results. I would like to see him face to face, as soon as you deem it safe, just to be certain, but I'm reasonably sure there's nothing magical about the man."

"That's a relief," Jake stated, letting go of his held breath. "I don't like the idea that we just got here and already someone is watching us. Ria's had enough of that sh— uh…stuff—to last a lifetime."

Jacki laughed at his obvious attempt to clean up his language, but she didn't comment on it. Jake was a good guy. It was obvious to Jacki that he was very much in love with his new mate despite the fact that Jake was only human. He had significant gifts in being able to see the future at times, but he was not a shapeshifter.

That had to have been hard for Ria to accept, seeing as how the other woman was the leader of the *pantera noir* shifter Clan. But then, Jacki was learning, mating was something even more special than she had always been led to believe. It was magical and…sacred. That was the way she felt about her ever-strengthening bonds with both of her mates.

"We'll get to the bottom of this, Jake," Geir promised in a firm voice. "You can leave it with us. If the prisoner hasn't seen your face yet, I advise you to stay in here and keep it that way." Jake looked like he wanted to argue. "For Ria's sake,"

Geir added, and Jake visibly backed down from whatever objection he had been going to make.

The human, Ben Steel, arrived at that moment, escorted by two Royal Guards who had been sent to meet him. He greeted the men with firm handshakes and low words, then turned to nod respectfully to Bettina and Jacki.

"Is this the guy?" Ben walked right up to the glass and took a hard look at the prisoner. "Damn careless of him to get caught. He knows what you are." Ben looked closer at the prisoner. "I've seen him before. I even met him once. Thought he was okay."

"You know him?" Jacki asked, surprised into speech though she could see everyone else was thinking the same thing.

Ben turned to face them. "I've met him. I don't know him well, but I remember the basics from his file. His name is Harper Sagtakos. He's from Long Island. Part Native American. Member of the tribe out there on the forks of the Island. Back when I started with the AC, I considered him for my team, but was guided away from him. That alone suggests he might be okay because the people I was guided toward instead, turned out to be traitors."

Silence met his words as everyone took in what he had said. Ben stood for a moment, clearly thinking, then spoke into the silence of the room.

"Let me talk to him. He'll remember me. Maybe I can find out what he was up to."

"Not alone," Bettina said at once. "We couldn't see any marks, but there's still a chance there's something hidden that I wouldn't sense from here."

Ben looked concerned. "I'm not sure, milady. I couldn't guarantee your safety."

Bettina laughed as she stood and walked over to Ben, taking his arm. "Don't worry about me, young man. I assure you, I can take care of myself."

She escorted him out the door and everyone turned to watch as the two entered the room on the other side of the glass. The prisoner looked up at the door, defiance in every line of his body until he got a good look at the two who had entered. Then he started cursing.

"Fuck, man, what the hell is going on here?"

"Easy, Harper. There's a lady present." Ben moved aside as Bettina strode past him, walking boldly up to the prisoner, looking him in the eye.

"Are you here to harm us, agent of the *Altor Custodis*?" she asked bluntly.

"If you know I'm *Altor Custodis*, then you know I'm only here to watch and observe," he replied. "Did he tell you my affiliation?" Harper nodded toward Ben.

"I know you are *Altor Custodis* from your mark," she stated, tapping his arm, just above the handcuff that kept him chained to the pipe in the corner.

"You're not human, are you?" Harper asked, seeming to become a bit more cautious.

Bettina laughed and the tinkling tone charmed everyone who heard it.

"Will you write that in your report to your AC bosses?" she asked, challenging him. Jacki held her breath as she watched the scene unfold on the other side of the glass.

Harper tilted his head, narrowing his eyes as he looked down at her. "Why shouldn't I?"

"Because you're a smart man," Ben interrupted, drawing his attention. "You should realize by now that the AC has been infiltrated by *Venifucus* agents. They used my reports to find and murder the people I'd been assigned to watch."

"You have proof?" Ben's expression looked open, if wary, not argumentative to Jacki's eyes.

Ben nodded slowly. "Sadly, yes. A trail of death followed my reports all across the country. I finally figured it out a few months ago."

Harper seemed to wrestle with his response. He kept quiet while everyone studied him. He also squirmed a little under Bettina's scrutiny, Jacki thought, but then again, who wouldn't? Bettina could be a very scary lady, despite her innocent appearance.

"Is that why you were so blatant here? Did you want to get caught?" Ben finally asked. The idea hadn't occurred to Jacki, but she could see Ben had hit a nerve when Harper stiffened and gripped the pipe harder. "Or is it a double fake. Are you really working for the *Venifucus* and wanted to get closer by being so inept it was inevitable you would be captured? I know your skills, Harper. I know you're not this much of an amateur. You wanted to get caught."

"If you know so much, why can't you tell the difference? One of your magical friends should be able to tell if I'm on the right side or not, shouldn't they?" Harper looked pissed to Jacki's eyes.

"Indeed I should," Bettina said in a strong voice that rang through the room. All action stopped as time stood still for a moment.

And then she spoke a word that even Jacki couldn't hear. Bettina's lips moved, but the magic of the word was so strong, it blocked out all sound for the moment of its utterance. Bettina had told her that a few very special words of high magic could do that, but she hadn't demonstrated. She'd said the power it took to use such words was not something to be squandered in demonstration. That Bettina thought the use of her strength was so important now said a lot.

For a split second, everything about every person Jacki could see was outlined in stark, glowing colors. It was like seeing auras around every single being. Jake was surrounded by an outline of greenish-blue, like a calm and peaceful ocean. Beau was a fiery orange, Geir a bright golden hue that matched his golden hair. Jacki herself seemed sort of purple, if she had to give the amethyst glow around her hands a name.

Ben Steel shone a bright, pure silvery-gray, while his friend Harper was surrounded in tones of earthy green, like a forest. But Bettina's aura was purest white, with little motes of prismatic sparkle that held every color of the rainbow and beyond.

Jacki sucked in a breath and in the next moment, the colors were gone.

"You carry no taint of evil about your person," Bettina declared, moving back from the prisoner to take a seat on one of the chairs in the room. "But I cannot know what is in your heart."

Jacki wanted to go to her mentor, but knew neither the men, nor Bettina, would appreciate her interrupting this right now. Jacki had to wait and let the situation play out.

Bettina turned to Ben. "It's your call, Mr. Steel, whether or not to unlock his cuffs."

Ben nodded to Bettina, then turned to look at the prisoner again. "What'll it be, Harper? Will you be civilized if I give you a little leeway? I can assure you that these people are on the right side of the coming conflict."

Harper's eyes narrowed, seeming to evaluate Ben's words. "Then you feel it too?" he finally asked. "Something's building. Has been for a while now. Something big is coming, and it doesn't feel right. It feels like bad mojo heading our way."

"Interesting that you should say that," Bettina murmured. Jacki could see that she had been weakened by the use of such powerful magic, but Bettina hid it pretty well. "I understand that you are Native American. How close are you to the land and the people?" she asked in a somewhat challenging tone Jacki had never heard from her before.

"I'm a New York Indian, ma'am," Harper answered with a shake of his head. "I was born and raised on Long Island. My land is the beach and the Pine Barrens. The ocean and the bays. My people are few, but we do our best to keep the traditions alive. I personally have a lot of respect for the elders and their ways. So I guess you could say I'm as close as I can be, having been born a twenty-first century Indian in a white man's world."

"Well, I think that's as honest a self-assessment as I've ever heard," Bettina commented, approval clear in her voice.

She looked back at Ben. "It's up to you. Do what you think is best."

"So how about it?" Ben asked Harper again. "Will you behave if I let you loose?"

Harper shrugged as if it didn't make any difference, but Jacki knew better.

"Why not?" he answered offhandedly. "I'm not here to fight with anyone. I just figured it was about time to make contact and find out what the hell is really going on."

Ben nodded and moved forward with the key. He unlocked the handcuffs and removed them completely, setting Harper free. He rubbed his wrists for a moment, then walked slowly, very deliberately, directly over to where Bettina sat. He shocked just about everyone by sinking to one knee in front of her and bowing his head.

Even Bettina seemed a little surprised at first, but she handled it well. She raised one hand and placed it on top of Harper's bowed head as if in benediction. She must have murmured something, but Jacki couldn't hear what she said. After a moment, Bettina removed her hand from his head and Harper stood again. He moved around the small table and took one of the two remaining seats in the room. Ben took the other.

"Mind telling me what that was all about?" Ben asked, nodding toward Bettina. The High Priestess's gentle smile gave away nothing.

"It's obvious to me that she's a holy woman," Harper said. "A shaman of this tribe, whatever they are. Tigers, I was told, but there seems to be more going on here than the briefing I got suggested."

"Before we get to that—*if* we get to that—we need to know if you've already started reporting back to your superiors in the AC." Ben got down to business.

"No, I haven't. And I won't. Not until I get a clearer picture of what exactly is going on. Things aren't adding up anymore, and I'm not really sure who I'm working for just lately. There was a shakeup at the top and assignments got shuffled. It was all very clandestine and quickly arranged. I was moved out here on very short notice and told to report to someone I've never heard of before." Harper made a disgusted face. "It smells really bad from where I'm standing, but I wasn't sure what to do about it until just recently. I'd been watching the tiger family for a couple of weeks, and then all this activity started happening higher on the mountain. New people coming in. New security measures. And my spidey senses were telling me that these folks were okay. I mean, they might be badass soldier-types with the latest technology in surveillance, but they all fussed over that little tiger kid and treated her as if she was a princess. They couldn't be all bad, right?"

"You went soft over a kid?" Ben smiled and shook his head. "How the mighty have fallen."

"Have you seen her? She looks a little like my sister's kid. They're about the same age," Harper added. "Cute as buttons, and not a bad bone in their body at that age. My sister calls it the age of innocence. She says that comes right before the terrible twos, but I can't imagine my little angel of a niece will turn into a two-year-old terrorist the way my sister claims."

Bettina laughed and the chiming tone lit up the room. "Give her time. All babies go through a cranky stage around that time, brought about by frustration more than anything else. Some handle it better than others, but they all go through it. You'll see."

"I refuse to believe it," Harper smiled back at Bettina, seeming to have formed a liking for the woman that was hard to miss.

"Okay, so you liked the way the new people interacted with the child," Ben said, bringing them back on track. "And you decided to get caught?"

"Well, it wasn't quite as thought-out as you're making it sound," Harper admitted. "I got a call from my new contact one day, pressuring me for information. I really didn't like his tone, so I didn't give him squat. But then I started thinking.

Something about this whole setup really bothered me. I headed out onto that back country road to clear my head. I got out there and just sat in my car for a while...thinking. I knew the clunker was leaking oil. And that's what pushed me over." He ran a hand through his straight, black hair. "I smoked some tobacco, which I'm sure they found, right?"

Ben nodded and Bettina's eyes brightened. "Tobacco is an offering to the Great Spirit," she whispered. Harper bowed his head in affirmation of her words.

"I asked for guidance and prayed I was doing the right thing by breaking cover. I figured if the tiger family was going to know I'd been on the road, I might as well go all the way. I moved the two cameras I'd hidden the week before down a few branches so they'd be easily spotted. Downloaded the week's worth of data, as per protocol, but didn't do anything with it. And I stomped around a bit for good measure, leaving some prints on the perimeter."

"Well then," Bettina said with a shrewd look on her face. "I'd say your prayer was answered. The question is, where do we go from here?"

CHAPTER ELEVEN

Jake looked at his phone, scrolling through a few messages while Bettina and Ben spoke to the man in the other room. Geir watched as Jake scanned the information he'd been sent via his smart phone. If his expression was anything to go by, Jake seemed to approve of what he read.

"Now would be a really good time for a vision," Jake muttered, shaking his head as he turned to the rest of the people still in the room. Jacki, Beau and Geir were beside him, but there was still a Royal Guard or two watching from near the doorway.

"Too bad it doesn't work that way, eh?" Geir said, moving closer to Jake's side.

Jake was the mate of the Nyx. If he'd been a shifter, his role as a leader among the Clan would be much clearer, but since Jake was human, it was hard to know exactly where he fit at the moment. That was something Geir had hoped would be clarified once they settled into their new home and figured out everyone's new roles. He'd thought they would have some downtime after the recent battle to figure things out, but it looked like fate had other ideas. They seemed to be hopping from crisis to crisis still.

Another thing Geir had hoped to figure out was his own role in the Clan. He had trained the Nyx's Guard for years now, but he hadn't been part of the contingent that traveled with her while she was on the run. They had decided early on that it would be best if he stayed in one place, coordinating replacements for Guards who were injured, died, or retired. Geir was in charge of making sure there was always a supply of people ready, willing and able to defend the Nyx.

But now that Ria's days of running were over, things had to change. Geir wanted a more active role at her side. He wanted to be the Guard Captain he had always aspired to be. He hadn't had time to approach Ria about it yet. He had thought they would have plenty of time once everyone had settled down on the mountain. And then this happened.

Between Geir's uncertainty regarding his authority to command the Royal Guard—even though he had trained each and every one of them—and the confusion surrounding Jake's role in the Clan—even though he had great magic of his own, but was human—Geir was having a hard time figuring out how to approach the situation.

Beau, it seemed, had no such problems. He came up on Jake's other side and folded his arms, staring through the glass at the captive.

"You should let Geir and me handle this guy," Beau proclaimed. "We can keep him here and keep an eye on him. Master Geir has trained enough recruits to know how to evaluate people, and I can back him up. We shouldn't let this guy near the Nyx, but we might be able to create another ally if we work with him now. If we let him go, it's a wasted opportunity."

Jake turned to look at Beau. "Were you reading over my shoulder, Marine?" Jake asked with only a teasing hint of accusation.

"No, sir," Beau was quick to reply. "Why?"

"The background Ria dug up on this guy says he's a champion martial artist." Jake looked rather pointedly at Geir.

"He has the look about him. Lean muscle mass. Not too bulky. Walks smoothly for a human," Geir agreed. "No wasted motion." Geir approved of the way the man carried himself from what little he'd seen. It might be interesting to see how he performed in the dojo.

"I think your plan has merit," Jake said, responding to Beau. "But I want a chance to work with him. I think he needs to know there are other humans that are working with the Clan by choice. It might make him more comfortable. And I want to get my own measure of the man." Jake looked hard at the man through the glass. "If Bettina gives the all clear, I'll leave him here with you, under Ben's care. Let's introduce him to tigers first in the form of you and Master Geir. Let him think this is still a tiger stronghold if we can. Watch him, and talk to him, today and tonight. I'll come along tomorrow for a workout. Don't tiptoe around me like you have been. I'm just one of the guys, okay?" Here Jake narrowed his gaze and gave both Beau and Geir a blast of clear disapproval.

Maybe Geir *had* been tiptoeing around Jake, as he put it. Geir hadn't really realized it, but it looked like Jake certainly had. When they had time, they were going to have to figure out everyone's roles in the Clan hierarchy. If even the human had noticed the unease that Geir thought he'd kept well hidden, then they had to make time to spell it all out.

Geir nodded solemnly. "My apologies. There will be no more tiptoeing." Geir had to smile at the dainty word. "Come to the dojo tomorrow and there might be some ass-kicking, but definitely no tiptoeing."

Jake struck his hand out for Geir to shake and grinned. "I'll drink to that. Damn it all, but you guys are going to have to figure out I'm not some delicate little flower. If I have to wipe the dojo floor with your ass, then I guess we'll just have to get on with it." Jake laughed and Geir understood the human was taking steps to assert himself. Good for him. Geir, for one, was glad. "I swear," Jake went on, "if one more of your Royal Guards tries to help me across the street like a little old lady, I'm going to have to start busting heads."

Beau burst out laughing and Geir turned to look at him. "Sorry, man. But Jake here has quite a rep in Spec Ops. Geir,

I think you and your guys have riled the beast. Now you're going to have to take the consequences."

Geir's eyebrows rose. "Really?" He looked at Jake, willing to play along with the joke. He knew a bit about Jake's true abilities. For a human, he was very well trained, but Beau seemed to think he was even better than Geir had thought. Geir was intrigued. "Maybe we'll try out a few things tomorrow. I'll look forward to learning if there's truth behind the reputation."

"Oh, man," Beau grinned. "This is gonna be fun."

Bettina gave her approval of Harper's continued presence on the mountain. She couldn't find any evidence of evil intent in him. In fact, she told Jacki privately, she suspected something quite the opposite about their new acquaintance.

They had left the men with Harper in the dojo interrogation room. When they'd left, Jake was still watching through the glass, but both Beau and Geir had gone into the room with Harper, and Ben had introduced them all. Questions had flown around the room about the inner workings of the *Altor Custodis* and it had sounded like Harper was giving them very specific information—names and places. A couple of the Guards in the observation room with Jake were taking notes, but Jacki also noticed there was a discrete pile of blinking electronics in one cupboard. Everything that happened in that other room was being recorded.

Jacki would've liked to go on listening to the information Harper was relating, but Bettina had insisted that they needed to do some work to prepare for the next spell she planned for that night. Tom was stable, but he needed a final push out of the unconscious state that persisted.

Much to her surprise, Bettina took her on a tour of what Jacki had assumed was just a regular kitchen garden, outside the back door of the house. As it turned out, there were a slew of medicinal and magical herbs planted there, alongside the vegetable and flower beds.

It was late in the year, but Bettina ran Jacki through each of the plants and its uses, gathering a basketful of green leaves and stems, some roots, and a handful of colorful berries. She spent more time teaching Jacki about each one after they went back into the kitchen and began preparing them for use in the spell they would work that night. Bettina showed her how to handle them and the prayers to speak over the workspace and the work.

Jacki learned an enormous amount about herbal magic that afternoon. She only prayed that what they were doing was going to be enough to bring her brother back to full consciousness. He still hadn't woken up.

They had made remarkable progress in stopping the degradation that had been happening to him. Bettina insisted they had saved his life and made a good start on bringing him back from the edge, but Jacki wanted her big brother back. All the way back. Healthy and whole.

She spent time with him in between her tasks, sitting by his bedside and talking to his caretakers. Tad and Mandy had been incredible. They had watched over him, providing the medical care for which they'd been trained. Jacki couldn't have asked for better people to help her brother and she knew she couldn't have cared for him as well by herself.

Bettina left the herbs they had cleaned and prepared to one side of the kitchen sink when they were done and then started in on dinner preparation. The everyday task helped settle Jacki's mind until Bettina mentioned the extra guest she expected would make a showing at their table that night.

"That Harper is a complex soul," Bettina said as she peeled a potato.

Jacki was frying several packages of chicken she had found in the freezer and defrosted. She used a pinch of rosemary to season them and a lemon butter sauce that was among her favorite flavors.

"Is he going to sleep here in the house?" Jacki asked. She wasn't too keen on the idea of the stranger being in the house while her brother was still so vulnerable.

"I imagine so, but don't worry. I'm going to ward his door and any windows in the room they give him. I think Tad is planning to go furry and prowl the halls tonight." Bettina chuckled and Jacki had an image in her mind of the human man coming face to face with a tiger in the middle of a darkened hallway.

"Do you really think it'll be safe?" Jacki had to ask. Her brother's safety was at stake.

"If all goes as I expect, Tom will be back among the conscious once we've finished our work tonight. I wouldn't be surprised if he makes a very quick recovery after that. He's had a lot of time to sleep while his physical wounds have healed. Now we need to heal what the magic did to him and between us, we should be able to manage it." Bettina smiled at her encouragingly. "Don't worry. I have a strange feeling that Harper is going to surprise us in good ways from here on out. Still waters run very deep with that one, and his deep belief in the Great Spirit counts in his favor, for the Goddess wears many guises and carries many names. In the final analysis, any being on the side of Light can be our ally. I have high hopes that Harper Sagtakos will be one of them."

"Besides," Beau said from the doorway that led to the front of the house. "Jake vouched for Ben and Ben is vouching for Harper."

Beau walked into the kitchen, followed by Geir. They had entered the house from the front and had most likely heard most of Jacki's conversation with Bettina. Beau paused to give Jacki a quick kiss on the temple on his way to the refrigerator. He grabbed a cola out of the bottom of the fridge for himself and tossed one to Geir, which he caught as he paused beside Jacki to give her a kiss as well.

"Do you really trust all this vouching for each other that's going on? They're all human," Jacki questioned, still a little uneasy.

"Well, we all know Jake is above reproach," Beau stated, taking the half-peeled potato from Bettina and gallantly taking over the menial task. "If his mating of Ria isn't enough, I should also remind you that your own brother knows and trusts Jake from way back."

"He does?" Geir asked, already at the sink, washing and snapping the ends off of the pile of green beans Jacki had left nearby.

"Tom was a Navy SEAL. Jake was a Marine Recon major. Tom was Jake's dive master. Taught him everything he knew about diving—in and out of gear," Beau supplied. "From all accounts, Jake is part fish, thanks to Tom's training. Heard he did a flawless dive off the command deck of Sam's yacht to impress all the selkies. They sure talked about it enough. None of them thought a mere human could execute a soundless entry from that great a height before Jake proved them wrong."

"I would've liked to see that," Geir added, tossing the prepared green beans into a pot as he went.

"So we start with Jake. He's cool," Beau reiterated. "Jake has known Ben for a long time. Ben Steel was *Altor Custodis*, but he came over to our side fully once he realized his work for the AC was being used to murder innocent shifters and vamps all across the country. His heart was in the right place, but his masters at the AC betrayed his trust and that's something—from all accounts—our new human friend could not abide. Since he was confronted with the truth, he has been firmly on our side. The Napa Valley Master vamp vouches for him, as do a bunch of shifter Clans on the West Coast. He's also a friend of Jake's and Jake trusted him enough to bring him in on the rescue mission when he went to save Ria's life a couple of weeks ago. Ben delivered on that mission, as we all know. He helped Ria's injured Guards to safety and medical help, then brought them to the rendez-vous in North Carolina. We all also know what happened next and how Ben fought on our side in the battle that followed."

"So Ben is okay," Jacki agreed. "But what about this Harper guy?"

"Well, that's where it gets tricky," Beau admitted. "Ben

says he's okay and won't try anything that could hurt any of us. And you did your own examination of his character, right, milady?" Beau nodded to Bettina, who was sitting at the table, listening to all this with a faint smile on her face.

"I did," she agreed. "And I think we should give him a chance, as I've tried to tell Jacki, but you can't blame her for being worried about her brother." Bettina stood and went over to Jacki, placing an arm around her shoulders. "It'll be all right, my dear. Let's eat, then do our best to put your worries to rest and restore your brother to health. You'll see. It'll all work out. Have a little faith."

They ate together, joined by Ben and Harper, who was allowed to walk around the property, as long as he had an escort. For now, that was Ben. Conversation at dinner was stilted at first, and Jacki's tension level was pretty high. She didn't want to make nice with the human. She just wanted to get on with the spell and get her brother back. Was that too much to ask?

"I'm sorry if my presence disturbs you," Harper said after the silence around the dinner table had dragged on a little too long. He was looking at Jacki and she was startled out of her worrisome thoughts about Tom and the spell they were going to attempt later, when the moon was higher in the sky.

"It does," Jacki said honestly. "But probably not entirely for the reason you think. My brother has been very ill and I'm protective of him. He's in this house and we're going to be working magic tonight to try to bring him out of an unconscious state he's been in for a few days now."

Harper frowned, his dark brows drawing together in concern. "I didn't know you had an injured man here. I'm sorry to have intruded on your troubling time." He seemed to think before going on. "Is there anything I can do to help?" He looked pointedly over at the drying herbs on the side of the sink. "I was wondering what the leaf collection was for, but now I realize. You're going to try to work herbal magic on him tonight?"

"What do you know of such things?" Bettina asked

quickly, seeming intrigued.

"I'm an Indian, ma'am," he answered with a soft grin. "I know a thing or two about herbs."

Bettina laughed outright, surprising Jacki. "Come off it, Harper. Don't play the stereotype with me. You had to have learned something somewhere to say the things you have. Who was it who taught you about herbal magic?"

Harper grinned, clearly taking no offense. "You caught me." His dark eyes twinkled at Bettina. "My grandmother is a wise woman, like you, ma'am. She took me under her wing when I was a boy and my friends and I thought it would be fun to have a mud fight in the middle of her herb garden. She whipped my butt and then made me spend the rest of the summer putting her garden back to rights. I had to mow her lawn too. At first, it was penance for having messed up her carefully tended plants, but after a while, I started to enjoy working in her backyard and conservatory. She figured it out and decided to teach me what she knew. After that, I spent every summer in her backyard, working alongside her and learning everything she knew."

"Your grandmother had a *conservatory?*" Beau asked, emphasizing the word.

"Just because I'm an Indian, doesn't mean I come from poverty. Grandma has an honest-to-goodness estate in Southampton on Long Island. She even has a pair of peacocks that wander the grounds making a racket at all hours."

"Sylvie!" Bettina said with wonder in her voice and a broad smile on her face. "I knew you looked familiar. You're Sylvie Harper's grandson!"

"I thought your first name was Harper," Jacki said in confusion.

"Grams didn't want her family name to die out completely, and my mother agreed." Harper shrugged.

"Sylvie Harper is one of the wisest women I know," Bettina declared, reaching into her pocket and pulling out a cell phone of all things. "Let's call her. I bet we can clear up

Jacki's worries once and for all."

Bettina connected the call and put it on the speaker. Everyone waited while it rang. On the third ring, a female voice answered.

"Sylvie, it's me, Bette. I've got you on speaker. How are you, dear?"

"Fine, fine. To what do I owe the pleasure? I haven't heard from you in a few weeks. Everything okay?" asked the friendly woman on the other end.

"We're all hanging in there," Bettina replied. "The reason for my call is that a young man showed up here and I think he belongs to you."

"A young man?" the woman on the other end of the line sounded intrigued.

"Hi Grams," Harper said from the other side of the table.

"Harper? Is that you? What have you gotten up to now? Are you giving Bette trouble?" The woman's voice sounded far from chastising. She seemed more amused than anything, and very friendly. Jacki liked her tone. She sounded like a nice lady.

"Yeah, it's me, Grams. I sort of inadvertently ran into one of your friends and *her* friends are a little suspicious of my motives for being here. Could you tell them I'm not the boogeyman, please?" Harper seemed to have a good relationship with his grandmother, but Jacki didn't know either of them. How was she to take the word of a disembodied voice over a telephone?

"If you ask me, she should lock you up and throw away the key. How dare you drop in on Bette unannounced? What have you been up to, young man?" Gone was the teasing tone, replaced by outraged grandma. Jacki started to really like the older lady.

"Thanks, Grams." Harper rolled his eyes and sat back.

"Don't you roll your eyes at me, Harper. Did he roll his eyes, Bette?" the woman asked with accusation in her tone.

"Why yes, I think he did, Sylvie," Bettina answered with a grin. She seemed to be getting a kick out of the entire conversation. "Don't worry, hon. Your misplaced grandson gave my friends a scare, but I think we've got him sorted out now. How much did you teach him about plants? Does he share your gift?"

There was a bit of silence on the other end of the line before the other woman answered. "You put me on the speaker," Sylvie reminded her friend. "Is everyone there trustworthy?"

"Those present include my apprentice and her mates," Bettina answered. "Your grandson has an old friend here as well, and seemed comfortable claiming herbalist knowledge in front of him. I'm assuming it's okay with you, Harper, that Ben now knows?" Bettina nodded toward the other human.

"It's fine with me," Harper replied. "We humans have to stick together."

"Bette!" Sylvie drew attention with her scandalized tone. "Did my impatient grandson infiltrate a group of shapeshifters? Harper! How could you?"

"It wasn't like that, Grams—" he began, trying to defend himself, but Bettina held up a hand to silence him.

"It's all right now, Sylvie, but I think you're going to have to have a long talk with your grandson about who to trust, and where to place his allegiances. He was working for the *Altor Custodis*."

"Harper!" The woman now sounded irate. And it was telling that she appeared to know all about shifters and the ancient organization of watchers. "How in the world did you get messed up with those idiots? We're going to have that long talk the minute you get back home, young man. I thought I taught you better than this. I'm very disappointed in you. Very disappointed."

Harper didn't look happy. In fact, if a grown man could look like a chastised school boy, he was doing a good impression of just that.

"I'm sorry, Grams. I wanted to know more, and you wouldn't tell me. I thought the AC was okay, but I finally figured out something was very wrong with the organization," he admitted in a low voice. "I let myself get caught rather than file a report."

"You silly boy," Sylvie chastised him, but Jacki could hear the love shining through her words. "I didn't tell you certain things for your own protection. Why couldn't you just trust me?"

"I do trust you, Grams. You know I do. I just..." he trailed off, shrugging, seeming unable to express himself further.

Sylvie sighed over the phone. "You were too impatient to wait for me to lift the ban on your further education, weren't you? I should have known when I didn't see you for so long." The woman paused before continuing. "Well, as long as Bette was there to catch you before you made an even bigger mistake, I suppose you got off lucky."

"I think more than luck was at work here, Sylvie," Bettina said softly. "I think maybe he was meant to be here, with us, at this time. We have a very sick man in this house. He's been drained by evil magic, which we managed to stop, but he still hasn't come all the way back to us. We're about to try a reunification spell tonight, at the moon's height. Does he truly know the Way?"

The woman was very serious when she answered. "He does. And he has a true and powerful gift, Bette. I taught him everything I know about herbal magic and he's experienced in its use." Then her tone turned more casual. "He can begin to make up for some of his stupidity by helping your sick man. And when you're done with him, I expect you to ship him back to me. I see there are still a few things I need to pound into his thick skull."

Bettina laughed. "Thank you, dear friend. It warms my heart to know that blood of your blood will be here to help us tonight. And I'll be more at ease knowing he comes from your family and has your teachings in his soul."

"He's a good boy, Bette. Willful, like most men, but kind-hearted and brave," Sylvie said about her grandson. "I'm sorry he met you in such a way. Eventually, I would have arranged a meeting under much more controlled circumstances, but I suppose the Great Spirit guides our path in ways we cannot always control. Something tells me he's where he needs to be at the moment." Conviction rang in her tone. "Just don't forget to send him back my way when you're done with him."

"Will do, my friend. For now, he's safe with us and learning first-hand about the world. Maybe he'll be able to show you a thing or two when he finally gets back." Bette laughed and the ladies exchanged a few more pleasantries before they finally ended the call with Harper promising to visit his grandmother as soon as he was able.

Jacki was charmed by the entire exchange and Harper seemed to take the inevitable ribbing from the other guys with good grace. At one point he teasingly declared that grandmothers were sacred and he dared any one of the other men to defy their own grandmothers. They all laughingly agreed to the premise that grandmothers could be scarier than drill sergeants and eventually let the subject drop.

By the time they were ready to do the spell later that evening, everyone was gathered in Tom's sickroom. Harper had been put through a bit of a quiz on the herbs they had gathered and Bettina had smiled in satisfaction when he passed her test with flying colors. She put the herbs in his care and let him take the lead on laying them out around Tom's prone body.

Bettina explained to Jacki that they had to be put in a certain order, in certain places. She offered a low-voiced narration as they watched Harper prepare the room.

"I was going to have you do this, because of your relationship with Tom, but it's best done by a warrior. Your energy is of healing and care. What we need here is a fighter, willing to battle for your brother's soul. Your mates will be of help there too, but I think the spell will be even more effective now that we have a warrior mage to lead it." Bettina watched Harper's actions with approval. She seemed very happy that he was there and Jacki hoped and prayed Bettina's enthusiasm would be rewarded with Tom's speedy recovery. Jacki wanted her big brother back.

After the herbs were laid out, Bettina spent a moment arranging the people in the room exactly where she wanted them. Harper was at the head of the bed, Bettina to one side between Tad and Mandy, with Jacki on the other, between her mates. Even Ben had been invited, standing at the foot of the bed with a sort of quasi-bewildered expression on his face.

When she had them all placed where she wanted them, Bettina spoke.

"What is the ceremony we are about to enact?" she asked, in ritual tones.

"We seek reunification of this man's spirit with his body. He is lost in darkness. We will show him the path back to the Light," Harper answered in a strong voice as Bettina smiled.

"We have quite a collection of warriors and healers here to witness and lend their strength to this gathering. Ben and Harper are the humans who ground us. Jacki and I are the priestesses that represent the Mother of All. Tad and Mandy are healers, but warriors as well and Master Geir and Beau are warriors, pure of heart and purpose. Tigers all, our shifter friends will connect with the wild side of Tom's selkie spirit, as will his sister's inner beast. It is a good balance of virtues and roles. Begin when you are ready, Harper." Bettina nodded toward the man standing above Tom's head, holding a sprig of mixed twigs and stems in his hands.

Harper began to chant, but it was in no language Jacki had ever heard before. She recognized the power in the syllables, though. He must be chanting in some ancient Native tongue that evoked the same elemental power as the magical words and chants that Bettina had been teaching her, just using a different language.

Jacki was fascinated by the guttural words that roused such immense magical power from the earth and sky, using them all as conduits. She recognized the goodness of the magic and any remaining worry in her heart was put at ease. Harper was doing good here. She could feel it.

Time passed. Jacki wasn't sure how much. They were all locked in place by the power of the chanted words. Bettina joined in and after a little while, Jacki got the hang of the foreign syllables as well, adding her voice to the chorus as the power swelled and built.

She could feel the drain on her own internal power but was glad to give of her own energies if it meant getting her brother back from the darkness. She could feel the power gathering at the head of the bed, shaped by Harper's words. It was a slow build, but when the crescendo was almost upon them, he chose the most opportune moment to loose all the energy he had gathered.

Jacki could almost see it flowing into her brother, seeking. Finding all the places inside him that were strangely empty, and…filling them with the combined goodness of all those present. She felt the way the power coaxed her brother's spirit—at first very far away, then slowly, painstakingly, growing closer and closer until…it was almost there.

The power rose and lassoed around Tom's spirit, taking it downward, away from the other realms and back into his earthly body. Tom jolted on the bed, but Harper reached forward, touching Tom's forehead with a sprig of evergreen, running the small bouquet of leaves and needles over him, pausing on certain key spots. The pulse points. The third eye. The chakra points. The meridians.

Little by little, her brother's spirit was reunified with his waiting body, sealed in place by the benevolent magic Harper had gathered and wielded with skill. He was definite in his movements and sure in his will. Jacki admired his power and the way in which he battled gently with Tom's powerful spirit, which seemed at times to not want to listen.

"It must be beautiful where he is, for him to fight so strongly against coming back," Ben muttered. It was then that Jacki knew they could all see what was happening. Powerful magic, indeed.

Harper looked up at them. "Call him back to you, Jacki. Make him listen. I have fought the battle with his spirit, but the rest must come from his heart. Only you can appeal to that, blood of his blood."

"Tommy, don't leave me," she whispered. Jacki reached out to take Tom's hand in hers, feeling her mates' hands on her shoulders—one on each side, lending her their strength. "Tom. I need you. Our family needs you. Our Clan needs you. Don't leave us here to fight the threatening darkness on our own. We need you here. Come all the way back to us." She could feel him wavering, not exactly consciously defying her pleas, but being tugged by forces she didn't understand to stay in the realm his spirit had hidden in for days now. "I love you, Tommy. Please don't leave me."

That did it. She felt him make up his mind as his spirit flowed back into his body, joining firmly and settling in his heart. Tom's eyes blinked open slowly as he looked around at the gathering with confusion.

"What is this? Some kind of intervention?" His voice was ragged with disuse, but he squeezed Jacki's hand even as he squeezed his eyes shut and seemed to try to regroup.

CHAPTER TWELVE

"How long was I out?" Tom asked when he opened his eyes again.

"Three days," Bettina answered in her lilting voice, drawing all eyes. "We have worked great magics to bring you back, Thomas. How do you feel?"

"Like I got run over by a truck," he answered raggedly. "A couple of times." He tried to sit up in the bed, but gave up after a quick, failed attempt. "Jack, sweetheart, is there any water?" He squeezed her hand again and she felt tears running down her face. He swore under his breath and tugged on her hand so she leaned over him. "Don't cry Jack-in-the-Box. I'm okay. Just thirsty."

"I'm so glad you're back." She punched his shoulder with no force at all. "Don't you ever scare me like that again, Tommy. Not ever."

"I'll try my best, Jacki-bean." He suffered her kisses on his cheeks and even wiped away her tears for a moment before Jacki became aware of all the people still in the room.

Tad held out a glass of water with a bendy straw in it. Jacki took it gratefully as Mandy reached down to stuff a few pillows behind Tom's back while Harper helped lift his shoulders so he could sit up a bit. When he was at a reasonable angle, she sat on his bedside and held the water glass out to him. He drank happily, seeming to enjoy each sip as his dark eyes examined every face in the room. His nose twitched too, so she knew he was sniffing out all the various beings.

"I guess you're wondering who some of these folks are," Jacki said as he continued to drain the glass. "Tad and Mandy are doctors. They helped take care of you. You know Ben, Bettina, Beau and Geir. This is Harper, a recent arrival. He led the final spell we did tonight to bring you all the way back. He's human, but we won't hold it against him." She smiled up at Harper, joy in her heart and great respect as well. "Thank you, Harper," she said softly. "You've given me a great gift, bringing my brother back to me."

Harper bowed his head in acknowledgment, but said nothing. Bettina took over and announced that she was leaving the room, since Tom was so much better. She took everyone with her except Jacki, Beau and Geir. When the door closed behind her, Tom frowned at Jacki.

"What's going on with these two guys and why are their energies blended with yours, Jack? What happened while I was out of it?"

He sounded suspicious and almost a little angry, but Jacki knew they were going to have to deal with this sooner or later. It seemed like Tom's walk on the spirit side had left him with some lingering effects if he could sense the energies around her and her mates, but she'd discuss that with Bettina tomorrow.

She had to face this head on. All at once. Like ripping off a bandage. She took a deep breath.

"They're my mates." She scrunched up her face, waiting for the explosion, but it didn't come. She hazarded a look at Tom's face and he seemed both a little stunned and a whole lot angry, though over it all was a wary sort of confusion. She decided to press on with the news. "And I'm in training to be the next High Priestess. I'm Bettina's apprentice, so she thinks that maybe the Goddess intended for me to have two mates—like Allie and the Lords—so I'll be better able to deal with taking over from Bettina, if I ever should have to do so."

That seemed to give Tom something to think about. He looked at each man appraisingly.

"Do you each love my sister?" he finally asked in a challenging tone.

"To the end of time," Geir answered without hesitation.

"All the way, man," Beau seconded, nodding. They stood at her back, ready to help her should she need it.

"And I love them. It's meant to be, Tom. Bettina saw it right away. It took the three of us a little longer to figure it out, but I think we're pretty much there now. I won't give them up. Either one of them. I can't. They are part of my soul, as I am part of theirs."

Bettina came back and shooed Jacki and her mates out of the room about an hour later. They'd filled Tom in on almost everything he had missed while he'd been ill. As the hour passed, he seemed much, much better. It was almost as if he was gaining strength before their eyes.

When Bettina escorted Jacki to the door, they had a quick conversation that reassured Jacki the High Priestess intended to do a thorough examination of her brother, and any lingering effects of his illness that might occur. Jacki told her that Tom had sensed the blending of energies around her and her guys, but Bettina didn't seem surprised. She only nodded and reassured Jacki that all would be well. Bettina would stay with Tom for as long as he needed looking after.

Jacki led the way to her bedroom with a weary sigh. She felt at peace about her brother's condition. He was on the road to a speedy recovery if the past hour was anything to go by.

She must have been standing in one spot for a little too long because the next thing she knew, Geir had put his arms around her from behind, settling his chin on her shoulder, his lips next to her ear.

"Are you too tired?" he whispered, but there was a growl underlying his words that meant his inner cat was coming out to play. She knew what that meant by now. Geir only ever really let his cat rule over his human form when he was making love to her.

"I'm never too tired for my mates," she replied, needing the comfort of their embrace as much as it sounded like Geir needed her.

He nipped her earlobe in approval and lifted her into the air, carrying her the rest of the way to the bed. He didn't put her on it, but rather, lowered her to her feet beside the bed, turning her so that he could kiss her. She got lost in his kiss. Geir was a really good kisser. Wild and untamed, yet gentle enough to really enjoy.

And then Beau came up behind her and began to tug at her clothes. Geir kept kissing her while both men—though mostly Beau—undressed her, bit by bit, until she was standing naked between them.

Geir continued to kiss her mouth, while Beau used his lips in other sensitive spots on her body. Four hands caressed her, delving into secret places and sliding over skin that was thirsty for their touch. She reached around behind her with one hand, stroking Beau through his clothes, while she did the same to Geir with her other hand.

Cupping them both, she realized again how lucky she was to have these two amazing men in her life. She really felt like she was getting away with something, but she'd be damned if she would regret it.

She broke away from Geir's hot kiss to complain. "You have too many clothes on"

Geir growled low in his throat and it was one of the sexiest sounds she had ever heard. Her inner selkie wanted to clap in excitement, but decided to wiggle against Geir's hard body instead. She wanted him skin to skin. The fabric between them was unacceptable.

She used a little bit of her upper body strength and pushed against Geir's shoulders until he collapsed down onto the bed. She followed after, straddling him until he was beneath her on the big bed. She remained on all fours, hands and knees, butt up in the air, while she sought out her target. Her mind was fixated on one thing—she wanted his pants off.

"It would be really handy to have claws right now," she murmured as she went to work on the button and zipper of his pants with her human fingers. Selkies had a lot of magic, but their beast halves weren't very useful on dry land sometimes. Put her in the water though…and watch out.

"No claws," Geir said quickly, the growl still very present in his sexy voice. "Delicate equipment."

That made her laugh, even as her body clamored for satisfaction. She wanted his cock and she wanted it now. No more delays.

Finally, her fingers found the right angle and his pants came undone. Geir lifted his hips, eager to help her reach her goal. And then there he was. Hard, hot, long and thick. Ready and waiting.

She grasped him in her hand and lowered her head toward him even as she heard the rasp of another zipper behind her. Glory be, Beau had figured out what she wanted and was moving to comply. She could see she was going to have to spend some time training her men, but she looked forward to it with an unbridled hunger for more.

She closed her mouth over Geir as she felt the heat of Beau approach from behind. She was kneeling very close to the edge of the mattress, so he had plenty of access to put himself where she most wanted him. She hoped—prayed— he'd come into her right away, but the tease decided to play a bit.

Jacki groaned around Geir's cock, eliciting a rumbling purr from his chest when Beau licked her pussy from behind, pausing to let his tongue dance in her folds, pushing her arousal even higher. She didn't think she could take much more. She wanted to be possessed as much as she was possessing. She wanted to be taken while she took, and gave in return.

But Beau had other plans. His tongue lapped at her while his fingers explored. She cried out, clenching around his fingers for a moment when he pushed her just a little too close to the edge. That drew a purr of satisfaction from behind her while she sucked hard on Geir, passing her pleasure on to him. Both of her big cats were purring now and she sensed a change in the air as Beau rose to his feet behind her.

Finally. Yes, dear Goddess, she was getting what she wanted. Beau pushed into her from behind and she relaxed into his possession, allowing him to set the pace. Her mouth relaxed on Geir, but didn't let him go. She wanted Beau to push her forward, stroke for stroke, as she let Geir slide down her throat.

He began to move. Oh, yeah, that was just what she thought would happen. Geir groaned as she took him deep, retreating as Beau retreated from her pussy, then going forward again. They were a well-orchestrated trio and Beau was in charge of the tempo, for now.

She felt the moment he realized it too. He clenched, coming into her hard, pushing her almost a little too fast, but then he backtracked, seeming to realize what he'd done. His pace was slow and steady from there on out, and his hands on her ass squeezed in appreciation as he went balls deep inside her over and over.

Eventually though, the climax rose to meet them all. Geir's hands were clenched in the bedding and she could see a bit of orange fur sprouting around his knuckles as his tiger began to take hold. Geir growled almost continuously as she took him deep, in time with Beau's faster thrusts. Beau's hands on her ass seemed to be tipped with sharper fingernails than she was used to as well. His beast was closer to the surface, hardening his fingernails, but Beau's human side was definitely in control. His pseudo-claws didn't break the skin, but they did add a level of excitement with the scratchy, hard touch that she hadn't expected.

When Beau's thrusts turned into sharp digs, she used her mouth and hands on Geir, sucking hard while she gripped the base of his cock. They were close now—all three of them.

And when the storm broke over them, it was simultaneous and incredibly satisfying as each of them cried out and came. Jacki's mouth lost its grip on Geir, but her hands stroked him as his come shot outward, bathing her chest with his tribute. She realized what he'd done when she felt his strong hands gripping her shoulders, holding her above and slightly away from him.

Even in his passion, he was looking after her. They all breathed hard as passion shook them up and wrung them out. She felt Beau come inside her, the jets of warmth making her feel amazing as her body jerked and shook in a heady release.

When it was over, Beau collapsed on one side of the big mattress while Geir took the other and positioned her between them. They lay there for long, satisfied moments, letting their thoughts drift. The men reached out to stroke her skin from time to time as she did them. The togetherness was new and lovely. Almost as satisfying as the intense orgasms her mates gave her.

"I'm sorry I almost lost it," Geir said after a long, quiet moment.

Jacki frowned. "Lost what? You were amazing, Geir." She put one of her hands on his arm, stroking lightly. "So were you, Beau. Nice rhythm and you didn't take long to figure out what I wanted you to do. A plus for effort," she teased him, stroking his arm with her other hand.

"I almost went tiger on you, Jacki. I'm sorry," Geir said, sounding both weary and disgusted with himself. "The only thing that stopped me was that I couldn't let you choke. I only just found enough reason to lift you away at the very last minute. You shouldn't have let me take so much advantage of your good nature."

"Is that what you think?" She rose up on one elbow, looking at him. "Seriously, Geir, I enjoyed every minute of what we just did. And if you hadn't lifted me up, I would've handled whatever you could dish out. We'll have to try it again until you figure that out." She grinned and moved to kiss him, but he held her back and she could see he really was upset.

"Jacki, you need to breathe," he reminded her in a chastising tone. "I don't want to hurt you. The cat just takes control and I'm so afraid he's going to do something my human side will regret forever."

"Whoa there, Geir," she said lightly, trying to soothe him. "First of all, you would never hurt me no matter what form you wear. I know that in my heart. In my soul. You should too. Don't doubt yourself. This mating is between not just our human sides, but our beasts as well. Your tiger chose my seal and vice versa. They know who and what we are at all times. They won't hurt each other no matter what. You've got to trust that." She stroked his hair with one hand and was glad when he allowed her touch. "As for breathing, you do realize I'm a selkie, right? I'm very at home underwater and we seals can hold our breath for a mighty long time. Do I have to prove it to you?"

Geir looked deep into her eyes and she saw the moment he let go of his worries—at least for now. He smiled at her, reaching up to cup her cheek with his palm.

"We'll have to make love in the water sometime," he said softly, purring once more. "I'd like to see this seal talent first hand."

"Oo-rah," Beau chimed in from the other side of the bed, in clear approval of the idea.

"Later," she promised them both. "It will be my pleasure, I'm sure." With a little giggle, she flopped down between them and basked a little more in the love of her new mates.

They got up eventually and cleaned up, but the guys ambushed her in the shower, eager for her to demonstrate some of her talents in a water environment—or so they claimed. What followed was a slippery, soapy romp that had them all alternately laughing and crying out in pleasure. Rumbles of sexy cat noises made her feel like a sex goddess for the first time in her life as her mates made sure that every millimeter of her body was cleaned and buffed to perfection—and to a great deal of pleasure.

Whatever hang-ups she might've still had about her body and her curves were laid to rest at the feet of her mates' enthusiasm. They proved to her over and over again that they loved her just the way she was, and she was finally beginning to believe it—to believe in herself. It was yet another gift of her mating with these two amazing men, and her newfound confidence in herself was something she would always treasure.

The next morning, Geir felt so much more balance in his being as he meditated before starting his day in the dojo. He hadn't had a lot of time to spend on actual training of his students since arriving in New York. Today, he hoped to start getting back to some kind of training schedule, now that more of his students were settling in here, and the active duty Royal Guards had begun using the dojo to work out while off duty.

Geir had posted a tentative class schedule on the door yesterday. When he'd arrived in the dojo shortly after dawn, he had been pleased to see a small group already there, warming up, only waiting for him to start the class.

This was the kind of life he enjoyed. Getting up at dawn to start his day with training and meditation before breakfast, then teaching and helping the next generation later in day, followed by whatever other tasks he needed to perform in the afternoon. If he had his way, and could talk Ria and Jake around, he hoped to round out his day with those he had trained—leading the Royal Guard—now that they were all in one place.

He was biding his time until the opportunity to discuss the possibility of expanding his role arose. Geir was a patient man. He could wait until the time was right. So much had been happening in the Clan over the last few weeks, everyone was still in a state of flux.

When Geir rose from his meditation, he wasn't all that surprised to find Beau already in the dojo, warming up on the mats with the others. A nice group of about a dozen experienced Guards were talking quietly as they stretched their muscles in preparation for Geir to start a class. He felt a sizzle of satisfaction run through his veins. This was the kind of life he had always wanted. A place for himself, where he could use his talents for fighting and teaching to the best of his ability, a home of his own, a mate, and the promise of a family in the future. Life really couldn't get much better than this.

Geir moved forward to lead the class with satisfaction running through his being. He put them all through their paces before splitting the group up into pairs for *kumite*— hand to hand sparring practice.

Geir watched and made corrections or suggestions to each group, eventually facing off with Beau in a match that taught him even more about the man who had somehow become part of his family. Beau was a quiet, thoughtful fighter. He was sly and silent, using the smallest opening to every advantage. Geir had known the skill behind Beau's movements all along, but to have it out in the open was both a challenge and a relief. Beau had been somewhat secretive up to this point, never really displaying his full set of skills publicly, unless in the heat of battle.

Geir was relieved that Beau was willing to expose his many strengths—and a few weaknesses as well—in front of the class. It meant that Beau was willing to become a full part of this Clan and he would be a welcome ally in helping keep Jacki safe.

Geir was challenged by Beau's unique fighting style, which was a tiny bit stealthier than Geir's own. He adapted well, though. It became clear to Geir, now that they weren't trying to pummel each other into dust, that if Beau ever wanted to compete for Geir's spot as Master of the Royal Guard, he would have a good shot at it.

Knowing that would keep Geir on his toes. Healthy competition was always a good thing. And a good second-in-command was an even better one. Yes, things would shape up nicely—if Geir had any say in the matter.

When the class ended and everyone went in their separate directions to start their days, Geir and Beau headed back to the house. Jacki met them at the kitchen door, the aroma of breakfast being cooked wafting toward them.

"Give us a minute to clean up and we'll help you with breakfast," Geir immediately volunteered, pausing only a moment to give Jacki a kiss on the cheek.

He was sweaty and in need of a shower, but that wouldn't take long. He high-tailed it down the hall to his room. Beau was right behind him, heading for his own room and attached bath. Even as he hopped into the shower, Geir thought about ways to modify the house so that they each had their own space, including two—possibly three—full bathrooms in their master suite.

He had never been so domestic before. He'd never had the luxury of owning a place he could change to suit his needs. Geir was putting down roots here in a big way, and he couldn't wait to talk over his ideas with his new family at breakfast. The day had only just begun, and it was already one of the best days of his life.

Geir had a feeling that every day with Jacki was going to feel this way. This was…happiness. Geir hadn't had much experience with that emotion in the past, but he felt like maybe he might just become an expert on the subject given enough time with Jacki as his mate. A lifetime ought to do it.

CHAPTER THIRTEEN

After their showers, Beau and Geir helped Jacki finish making breakfast. The rest of the big house's current residents joined them—including a much-improved Tom. The big kitchen table was full this morning, with Mandy, Tad, and their little daughter, plus Tom, Harper, Ben and Bettina.

Conversation was loud and friendly, and huge amounts of food were consumed. Beau felt at home for possibly the first time since his parents' deaths. This big, open place was nothing he ever could have imagined, but everything he wanted in life. His mate. A home of their own. A place to use his talents for kicking ass.

It was a good life he could see unfolding before him. A really good life. Like nothing he ever could have imagined would come to him. Beau had half-figured he would die in battle someday, unsung and easily forgotten. Instead, here he was with the woman of his dreams, a fighting partner who was beginning to recognize that Beau had skills to offer in the dojo, and a mission he could get behind. Keeping the Nyx safe was something he could really *do*.

Beau had never really considered becoming a Royal Guard for any of the shifter monarchy. For one thing, until very recently, the tiger ruler had been a rat bastard, not worthy of the title. For another, Beau had chosen the mercenary road long before he truly understood the workings of the spiritual world, and the deep connection the true shifter monarchy had to the Lady and the Light.

Being older and wiser now, Beau almost regretted some of the things he had gotten himself into over the years, but he had to chalk it all up to experience. He had needed to do those things in those places to be ready for all that was presented before him now. He was the sum of his life experiences and all those questionable decisions had ultimately led him to the right place, so he figured he couldn't complain too much.

"I'm going with you when you head back to the dojo," Jacki said toward the end of the meal. "Some of the girls are going to work out this morning, right Mandy?" Jacki sought backup from the tiger female seated across the table. Both women were smiling as if they had something up their sleeves.

"Oh yeah," Mandy agreed readily. "Wouldn't miss it. I've been cooped up in the house for a bit too long. It'll be nice to stretch a bit."

Geir looked thoughtful when Beau shot him a questioning look. "I hadn't planned on segregated classes, but it's definitely something we can look into. There's plenty of space in the dojo at the moment—and there will be until more of our people get here," Geir finally said.

Beau realized Geir was being a little careful in his choice of words because of the humans listening in. Even though Harper and Ben seemed like good guys, the *pantera noir* Clan was one of the most secretive of all shifter Clans. Handing out even innocuous information easily didn't come naturally to someone who had been part of the Clan for so long.

"You guys are coming to the dojo too, right?" Beau asked innocently, knowing that Jake had planned to make an appearance this morning to check Harper out.

"Sure, why not?" Ben answered. "Looks like a really nice facility and I'm always up for a workout. Not sure I'll be able to keep up with some of you guys though," he said with a respectful bow of his head. "I'm only human, after all."

"I call bullshit, Ben," Tom piped up from the end of the table. "You're a SEAL. Human, as may be, but you've trained with my folk all along, even if you didn't realize it."

"Are you serious?" Harper finally asked. "Shifters are in the Navy? Navy SEALs are really tigers?"

Tom seemed to consider how to answer for a moment. "Some are tigers, yeah. But I'm a selkie. A seal SEAL. As I keep saying, we like the irony."

"No way. I thought you were all tiger shifters," Harper seemed really surprised.

"Did we ever say that?" Geir asked quietly, finishing his meal. "*Most* of us are tigers, yes. But there are a few who are Other things." Geir looked at Bettina. "How much should we tell him?"

Bettina just smiled. "His granny knows it all, Geir. More than any other non-shifter I know, in fact. She's not just some wise woman. She's the head honcho of all Native American wise women in the States. She is the keeper of wisdom from ancient times, and has held the post most of her unnaturally long life. I've known her for about seventy years, and she was old even back then."

"She's not really your granny, is she?" Beau asked, suspecting something greater was at work here.

"She is my blood. There just might be a few generations between her and me," Harper admitted, then turned to Bettina. "You really knew her that long ago?" He didn't really wait for her to answer. "Then you're not a shifter. You're something more…"

"What did Sylvie say to you about her origins?" Bettina asked instead of answering his statement.

"She said that her mother was fey. That makes Grams half-fey and very long-lived. As the subsequent generations mated with humans, the influence of the fey blood has diluted. I don't expect to live as long as Grams, but I will probably live longer than most humans, as all my relatives have done for hundreds of years thanks to Grams' blood in our lineage."

"You are part fey," Bettina confirmed. "That's the source of your very pure magic. And I am guessing that you're one of the most magically talented of your generation, which is why Sylvie took you under her wing. Right?" Harper nodded, but didn't speak. "I also have fey blood. A bit closer to the source than you, of course," Bettina winked at Harper. "It's not something I go around admitting to people just for the fun of it, you understand," she went on. "The Lords know. Many others guess. But I never really talk about it. I figured since we shared the blood of distant realms, you deserved to know for certain, Harper. And I let the rest of you in on my little secret—though it's not much of a secret at this point—because I think there's something special about this core group. I'm not sure what it is yet, but the more I contemplate the makeup of this little collection of shifters and humans, the more I think you were all brought together for a purpose. What that purpose is, I'm not sure yet, but perhaps it will come clear in time." Bettina shrugged and went back to finishing her breakfast as if she hadn't just dropped a colossal bomb on the entire gathering.

Beau said nothing but shot Geir a look. They both shrugged and went back to eating. Within moments, everyone had finished and the cleanup of the kitchen began. With everyone lending a hand—except Tom, who was ordered to sit and rest—the work went fast.

"What time is the next class, Master Geir?" Tad asked with a twinkle in his eye that wasn't lost on Beau. The tiger shifter knew what was on the agenda when Jake planned to confront Harper on the mats later this afternoon.

As far as the people in the kitchen were concerned, Harper had already proven himself by helping save Tom. The proof of his lineage had satisfied Bettina and went a long way toward convincing everybody else who'd heard that phone call with his grandmother, that he was okay. But Jake hadn't heard the call. And he hadn't seen Harper in action last night, saving Tom's life and strengthening his spirit. Jake still needed convincing, and they already had a plan in place for Jake to take Harper's measure.

Beau was looking forward to it, as were the others who knew about it. Harper, of course, knew nothing of the test to come, but he seemed calm and ready for just about anything. The rest of the day promised to be amusing.

"I don't do any physical training directly after meals, but it's a good time to work on tactics and less physical skills," Geir told Tad as they finished clearing the plates. "I'm still working out the schedule, but I'm thinking of doing a tactics class once or twice a week, followed by a beginner's class. Alternate days might have meetings or private sessions in those time slots. For today, since we still haven't ironed out who's here, who's coming, and what they all need in the way of classes and physical training, I'd like to do some of those assessments, then maybe get a group together for sparring in the dojo until lunch."

"I'd be happy to go over the training schedule my father worked out when the dojo was his, if that's any help," Tad volunteered. "I can also show you a little more about where things are kept in the dojo building. There are a lot of nooks and crannies built into the space that you probably haven't found yet."

And so it was, a couple of hours later, Beau found himself sitting near the door of the old barn that had been turned into a state of the art dojo, watching the ladies tumble and balance their way across the beams that ran the length of the building. The balance beams were even curved in spots, providing practice on a whole different set of skills. Beau was truly impressed by Mandy's agility. She had, of course, trained in this dojo all her life. It was clear she was quite a warrior in addition to being a protective mama.

Mandy's little girl was toddling along behind her, sure-footed as any cub, doing surprisingly good little cartwheels on the ground while her mother did back flips and shadow strikes on the beam above the little girl's head. Beau found himself watching the cub, wondering if Jacki's child would be as active and adorable.

It sort of struck him that he was thinking about having a family. Him. A man who hadn't had a home in longer than he could remember. It brought a tear to his eye that he quickly blinked back. He didn't want to have to try to explain the depth of his revelation to anyone, and he was surrounded at the moment by other spectators.

Ben had arrived with Harper a few minutes ago. They were dressed for a workout. Likewise, Tad was ready and waiting, coaching his daughter from the sidelines as his wife finished her gymnastics routine. The little girl would run into her father's open arms every few minutes, then run back to tumble around on the mats near her mother a little more. With the exuberance of the very young, she did this over and over, never seeming to tire of the game until her mother jumped off the beam with a spinning, twisting somersault, to land elegantly on her feet.

Mandy scooped the giggling little girl into her arms and walked off the mats, to her waiting mate.

"They look really happy," Ben observed with approval clear in his voice.

"The mate bond is strong," Beau replied with a grin. "And their cub lights up the room with her joy."

"Damn, man, you're getting to be a philosopher in your old age," Ben joked, then sobered. "But yeah, I see what you mean. I've seen it before among other shifters and even vamps, when they find their One. It's something to behold."

"I've never mixed with bloodsuckers much," Beau admitted, curious about the human warrior's experiences with vampires.

"Some of them aren't bad at all. In fact, they're pretty nice people, once you get to know them," Ben said. "Which doesn't mean they don't have their bad eggs in the group from time to time. I've just been pretty lucky with the ones I've met so far."

Geir came out of the small office in the back of the dojo,

which was the signal that the men were about to take the floor. The ladies had all finished their various exercise routines that weren't necessarily martial arts-based.

The fighting practice would come later and the classes wouldn't be segregated. Women would train to fight alongside the men because in the real world you couldn't always choose your opponent. An enemy might be male or female, shifter or human, mage or vamp. They had to prepare as best they could for any and every opponent they might face. This little morning dojo takeover was just a way for the ladies who hadn't been able to stretch their legs in a bit to get some exercise.

Jacki had participated off to one side in the big room, lifting weights, much to Beau's surprise. She could bench press almost as much as he could, which was another surprise. Apparently selkies had very strong arms and legs because, as Tom had told Beau, when in seal form, their flippers and muscles were what they relied on to help propel them through the water.

She finished off her weight routine with a stretching session that had Beau craning his neck as she bent almost completely in half—backwards. She was limber, was his little mate. He would have to remember that and put it to good use the next time they were making love.

He watched her as she came over to sit at his side, in the space between Beau and her brother, Tom. She squeezed both their hands, grinning from ear to ear. She was happy and the feeling was contagious. Beau brought her hand to his lips and kissed the back of it before he got up to join Geir. It was time to spar with the other half of the Royal Guard contingent.

They had just arrived with one very important human in their midst. Jake was here and Beau did his best not to stare as Harper was introduced. As far as Harper knew at this point, Jake was just another of the strange new inhabitants of the mountain. Their guest would learn soon enough that Jake's word was law up here and Harper was about to be put through a very thorough assessment by a man who had trained his human body to perfection...and beyond.

Even Beau was impressed with Jake's skills, and that was really saying something. Jake was a natural leader of men and had often assessed the warriors who were considered for his team when he'd been in the service. This wasn't Jake's first rodeo, and he would be able to learn more about Harper simply from the way he fought and defended himself than most men could learn with a full-on lie detector test. Harper didn't have a clue what he was in for.

Beau smiled as he took his place on the floor, standing next to Geir. He watched the others approach with anticipation. *Oh, yeah...* Let the games begin.

Jacki almost felt sorry for Harper when Jake took the floor opposite him for a sparring session. Almost.

She was sitting next to her big brother, at the back of the dojo near the barn door. A small set of bleachers had been set up back there for those who wanted to observe, and they were close to full as everyone who didn't need to be somewhere else at the moment seemed to sneak in to watch the match.

The rest of the class that had started out sparring with each other were gathered around, standing in a semi-circle on the mats as the two men faced off. Harper might've sensed that something was up from the way everyone was watching, but he didn't let it show. Jacki gave him a little tick in the plus column for that.

"Watch how Jake works around his guard," Tom whispered next to her. "He's a master at the bait and switch. He'll draw his opponent out just so far and then...blam." Tom's expletive coincided with a roundhouse kick that scored a definite point on Harper's midsection. "Damn, he's gotten better since we trained together in the service," Tom went on. It was clear her older brother admired the human who had just become the effective king of the *pantera noir* Clan by mating its queen.

Speaking of whom… Ria sat down next to Jacki, passing a bag of popcorn around. Jacki tried not to giggle as she munched on a few pieces of the salty snack and passed it back.

"How much did I miss?" Ria asked. The Nyx was not the kind of queen who stood on a lot of ceremony. She was very down to earth and Jacki respected her a lot.

"Not much. They just started," Jacki replied.

"Oh, good," Ria replied, munching away on the popcorn she'd brought with her. Jacki saw her cringe and she realized Harper had gotten a punch in past Jake's guard while she hadn't been looking.

"Good move," Tom commented. "If Jake has any weakness, it's that left hand. Occasionally—very occasionally—he drops his guard on the left. Harper is pretty good to have noticed it so early in the fight."

"You knew Jake before I met him." Ria said to Tom, talking quietly over Jacki, who sat between them. "He said you taught him to dive, but did you also train or fight together?"

"We were always training in the service," Tom confirmed. "And when Jake was part of my team, he fought and trained alongside me and my men. We were all selkies. Jake was our token human on assignment only for a couple of months, but he never kept us waiting. He was just as good as any one of us and if he had any deficits, he worked on them until they were strengths. I've never met a human more dedicated to being all he could be," Tom mused with a smile. "Jake's the real deal."

"I don't know," one of the others leaned in from his seat in the row above. "That Harper guy has some moves."

"Wanna bet?" Tom asked quickly, and within a moment he had quite a little pile of money and favors riding on Jake's victory.

From that point on the observers were quietly rooting for one or the other of the men. Jake kept Harper on the mats for the better part of an hour, drawing him out and making him work for every point he scored. By the end of the match it became clear that Jake could have ended it at any time he chose. He had been playing with the other man—testing him.

And Harper's reaction when he realized what was going on was gratifying. The man simply laughed and shook Jake's hand in respect and friendship. Harper didn't seem to mind he'd been evaluated and schooled by someone with more knowledge and experience than he in the art of hand-to-hand combat. If anything, he looked like he'd enjoyed the intense battle.

Tom collected his winnings with a broad smile and Ria's pride in her mate's skill was clear. She didn't seem to mind that some of her Guards had bet against her new mate. They'd lost their cash, or some kind of favor now owed to Tom, for their lack of faith in the Nyx's choice of mate. And they had learned a hard lesson. Each one of them looked at Jake with new respect.

The class broke up after a few more minutes and the group dispersed. Jake and Harper walked with Geir and Ben toward the bleachers at the back of the dojo. Geir grabbed some of the towels that were stacked to one side and threw a clean one at each of the guys.

Ria stood and went to her mate, reaching up to kiss his cheek as he put one arm around her waist. They looked so happy together, Jacki was touched by the deep emotions of love and caring both wore so openly on their faces. She wondered if she and her new mates looked the same and figured they probably did, but she didn't mind. She was too happy to not want the world to know.

She reached out and took both Geir and Beau's hands as they offered to help steady her as she climbed down from the bleachers. She didn't really need their assistance, but it felt good to have them fuss over her a little. The small gesture spoke of their care for her safety and comfort, which was yet another expression of the love they shared.

She let them draw her between them while Tom climbed down, still a little unsteady on his feet. He probably could have used a helping hand, but Jacki knew better than to offer. Her stubbornly independent brother would rather fall than admit weakness. She just intended to stick close to him while he healed so she could catch him if he fell.

"Do you want to stay for lunch?" Jacki asked Ria and Jake. "Bettina was making something that smelled wonderful when I left the house, but she refused to let me peek. She said to ask you to join us, if you have the time."

Ria looked up at her mate before answering. "We'd love to. Thanks for the invite."

"You're welcome anytime," Geir said formally though a smile lit his face as they all started walking out of the dojo. "You can use one of the guest rooms to clean up a bit if you like, Jake. I can loan you a change of clothes."

"Thanks," Jake replied. "I'll take you up on that."

It was only about twenty minutes later that they all reconvened in the formal dining room. A couple of the Royal Guard had been drafted by Bettina to help carry in an array of covered dishes from the kitchen. Heavenly aromas were wafting around the table, but Bettina made everyone sit still for her blessing before she would let anyone attack the platters of food.

Though it wasn't done at every meal, often a prayer would be offered up to the Mother of All for special occasions. Bettina declared this lunch a special occasion and spent a moment offering thanks and praying for continued blessings on all those gathered and all those who opposed the darkness. She specifically mentioned their allies, old and new, with a significant look in Harper's direction.

He had been told to sit, by Bettina, at one end of the massive, oval table. She was at the other end. When she held her hands out in the final part of her blessing, it was clear she wanted Harper to do the same. Standing, he matched her pose and the arc of rainbow light that passed from each of their hands, to the other, encompassed the entire table and all those who sat around it. Clearly, some kind of magical kick had just been added to the blessing by the presence of two powerful fey-blooded magic users.

The colors faded after a timeless moment and the two lowered their hands, sharing a look of pleased wonder across the length of the table. Bettina smiled knowingly. Harper just tilted his head as he grinned back at her.

"Thank you," Jake interrupted the moment, speaking loudly into the somewhat stunned silence. "You just cleared up a few things and now it all makes sense."

"What does?" Harper asked, looking at the man who had whooped his butt in the dojo not an hour before.

"His vision," Ria responded, lifting one of the covers off the platters in front of her. She licked her lips, clearly hungry and not willing to wait to dive into the food. "Jake sees the future. He saw something extra powerful—and confusing—this morning."

"You're a seer?" Harper looked at him with even more respect, if Jacki was any judge. "I thought you were a tiger shifter."

Jake laughed outright at that. "Sorry to disappoint you. I'm as human as you are. Maybe more human, judging by what I just saw, actually." Jake looked at the other man consideringly. "I just have a little gift."

"It's not little," Ria put in helpfully, making Beau guffaw at the unintended double entendre from Jake's mate. "What I mean is…" Ria said, shot a comedic, quelling look at Beau, "…his gift is actually rather large."

"I bet that's what he told you to say if anyone ever asked," Beau charged, still laughing.

"Dammit, Beau!" Ria lobbed a bread roll at his head. Beau caught in midair and promptly took a huge bite out of it, grinning all the while.

"Thanks, milady," he said around a mouthful of roll.

Jacki punched him in the arm and turned to Ria. "Ignore him. I'm still trying to house train him."

"Hey!" Beau groused, but it was clear he was enjoying the laughter, even if he'd become the butt of the joke.

"Harper, Jake is human with a gift of foresight. Other than that, he's not magical. Apparently, human magic users make him sneeze," Jacki added helpfully.

"And itch," Jake added, forking a huge slab of meat onto his mate's plate, serving her first, before he served himself.

It was so sweet to see him take care of Ria, Jacki thought. The Nyx deserved every attentive moment of her mate's presence in her life. She'd had it so hard to this point. They both deserved the obvious happiness they found in caring for each other.

"I saw you as a mage who wasn't one of those who make me break out in hives, but I didn't really recognize what you were. After the little light show, I understand now. You're like Bettina. Touched by the fey realm," Jake said matter-of-factly.

Harper looked stunned as he retook his seat. "Forgive me, but until I met Bettina, that was a closely held secret in my family. It's a little weird to be talking about it so freely here."

"Get used to it," Jake advised. "I've seen some weird sh—stuff—in my military career, but nothing compares to what I've seen in the weeks since joining my life to Ria's."

"You're mated, then?" Harper asked.

"Isn't it obvious?" Ria replied to his question with one of her own, taking Jake's hand in hers.

"Not to a human, love. They don't have matings that last for a lifetime all that often anymore. They no longer recognize the signs. At least, that's my personal theory." Jake shrugged as they all dug into their lunch.

Bettina sat and poured a glass of juice for herself. "That's really an excellent theory, Jake." The High Priestess looked impressed if Jacki was reading her right. "What Harper also fails to grasp is exactly who you are, Ria. I think the time has come to tell him all."

Jake squeezed Ria's hand. "She's right. The vision showed me this. He needs to know."

Ria looked unsure, but took a deep breath and faced Harper. "Like you and your secret heritage, I too have a secret," she began. She took another deep breath before her revelation. "I'm the Nyx."

CHAPTER FOURTEEN

Master Geir stood ready to deal with any sort of reaction to Ria's news, but Harper surprised him by saying nothing for a very long moment. Silence reigned around the table and all eyes were tuned to him.

"My grandmother told me about the Nyx of the shifter world. She said the Nyx held great responsibility, ferrying messages from the next realm to those in this one. It is an ancient and weighty responsibility and the woman who bears that burden is a woman like no other." Harper sounded as if he was reciting the words as told to him, verbatim. Perhaps he was. Either way, it sounded like he had a better grasp on the Nyx's role than most.

Ria smiled to hide a bit of discomfort, Geir could see. "Well, here I am. I hope you're not disappointed."

"Far from it, my lady," Harper answered formally. "I'm honored to meet you and even more honored that you were willing to reveal yourself to me, knowing that until very recently I was working for those who could seek to harm you."

"Yeah…about that," Ria began. "I know you were working for the *Altor Custodis*. And I know—I have proof from the Lords of North America—that the AC is corrupt at the highest levels. Knowing both those things, we have a proposition for you." Here, she looked at Jake and he took up the verbal baton.

"My vision showed me that your masters in the AC have no idea you have fey blood," Jake began, clearly waiting for a response though his statement hadn't been phrased as a question.

Harper nodded. "They don't know. My blood is so dilute, it's hard for human mages to discern—or so Grams claims. I fly under the radar ninety-nine percent of the time."

"And you haven't yet broken ties with the *Altor Custodis*, have you?" Jake went on.

Geir began to suspect where this was going and every muscle in his body tensed. He could see Beau had the same reaction, as did most of the men around the table.

"Wait a minute, Jake—" Ben protested, but Harper held up one hand, palm outward, gently silencing the other human.

"You want me to be a double agent?" Harper asked, seeming to mull over the idea for a moment.

"We've been on the defensive for way too long," Ria said, shaking her head. "We need to be proactive, not reactive."

"Your presence here presents a unique opportunity," Jake added. "For the first time, we could have eyes and ears inside the AC. Ben's intel has been invaluable from all accounts, but he burned his bridges with the AC. We haven't had any new intel on them in a long time." Ben shook his head, clearly uncomfortable, but Jake gestured toward him. "And that's okay, Ben. Don't beat yourself up about it. We have a chance here to do something more to clean up the AC, and I think we really need to think about taking it. If you're willing, Harper. It's all up to you. We can't force you to do anything."

Harper was silent for a moment before he focused his gaze on Jake. "How can you trust me?"

Bettina shattered the tense moment by laughing. "Are you kidding? Your grandmother would smite you all the way from Long Island to Timbuktu if you did anything stupid."

Harper grinned and ducked his head. "Anything *else*

stupid," he agreed. "She's still going to kick my butt for getting involved with the AC in the first place."

"Why did you?" Bettina pushed for an answer to the question that had been bothering Geir all along.

Harper looked around the table. "I wanted to *know*," he answered simply. "My grandmother has been a little stingy with the sharing of information on topics she fears might get me into trouble. I've always been fascinated by shapeshifters and she's always been reluctant to tell me more about them. I knew she had first-hand knowledge. I've seen some of her friends come and go from her estate and knew the exotic animals running around the grounds weren't just animals. They were her friends, being themselves in the safe place she had built around herself. But she never let me near them and I always wondered why."

"Why?" Jake said into the silence. "I can tell you why. She doesn't want to lose you, and she knows as well as I do that you are meant to mate with a shifter. When, who or how, I can't say, but I definitely see a fur-clad lady in your future, that's for certain."

"Seriously?" Harper smiled and his expression turned from wonder to cunning amusement. "The crafty old biddy! No wonder she kept me in the dark."

"Be careful what you say about Sylvie, young man," Bettina said with a comedic glare in his direction. "She's one of my oldest friends."

"So you see, if you turn traitor on shapeshifters, you condemn your own future," Jake went on. "I know you're smarter than that. And if you want to hang around with shapeshifters, you can get your fill in our Clan, right sweetheart?" Jake nuzzled Ria's cheek for a moment.

"You're welcome among the *pantera noir* Clan, Harper Sagtakos, as long as you remain on the side of Light," Ria said formally and everyone at the table stilled. The welcome of the Nyx meant something. Something important.

Harper seemed to realize it too. "I am honored," he said, sobering, one hand over his heart. "And I will do my best to live up to your expectations. If I may, I'd like to think about the idea of being a double agent overnight. I'll give you my answer in the morning."

"A sensible response," Bettina approved as she forked up a mouthful of salad and took a bite.

Everyone began to move again, eating and enjoying the meal. The talk turned to more mundane things like the way Geir intended to structure the classes in the dojo and how many students he could handle at one time. Eventually, Geir saw an opening to speak of something he had wanted to bring up with the royal couple for a while.

"You know, Beau and I are pretty evenly matched hand-to-hand. He has a unique style of fighting that may be of benefit to a few of our people. I'd like to add him as my second, if it's okay with you, milady," Geir asked respectfully.

Ria looked at Beau. "Have you guys straightened things out with the Kinkaid Clan yet? I assume you're staying here, right?"

Beau looked at Jacki and Jacki looked at Tom. Only Tom seemed uncomfortable. Jacki's decision had been made and Beau would go wherever she did, Geir knew.

"Not formally," Beau replied. "But we've decided to stay here with Geir, as long as we have your approval. In due course, Jacki and I would like to join *pantera noir*, even though we're neither *pantera*, nor *noir*," he joked.

Jacki touched his arm. "Speak for yourself. I'm almost *noir* when I'm in my fur. I'm sort of dark, gray-brown, which is closer to black than your orange stripes." She stopped fussing at Beau and turned to look at Geir. "Beau and I both know how precious your role is here, Geir, and how much you love your new house." She indicated the house around them with a sweeping gesture. "We want to help you make this house a home, and we hope we can find some useful role within the Clan, as the Goddess wills it."

Geir was truly touched. He reached out to take Jacki's hand, bending down to kiss her quickly. Beau gripped his other hand and when he rose, they exchanged a smile that meant the world to him.

"Well, that's settled," Ria broke into his happy moment with her amused voice. "And while we're at it, we have a few more things to settle." She paused, appearing to wait for him to look at her. "Master Geir, for years now you have trained my Royal Guard, always being certain I had the best of protection while I ran from my enemies. Your good work saved my life many times over and I cannot ever thank you enough for your dedication and skill. Each and every *pantera noir* Royal Guard working today is a product of your teaching and guidance, and they all look up to you as their mentor. Which is why, now that I'm no longer living the life of a fugitive, forever on the run, that I would like you to take over the role of Captain of the Guard in addition to your duties of Master of the dojo."

Geir was stunned speechless. It's what he'd wanted all along, but had been biding his time to find a way to discuss. It seemed the time had come and he hadn't even been aware of it until Ria seized the moment for him. Thank the Mother of All.

"I most humbly accept, milady." Geir bowed his head, holding her gaze as his heart filled with joy.

"I know it's a big job for one man to handle, which is why I would like Beau to be your second-in-command. He may be new to the Clan, but he's already a favorite among the warriors. His humor and skill will add to our Clan and as he is your partner in mated life, so he should be your partner in work. Or is that too much togetherness for you?" Ria broke the serious tone of her words with the humorous question.

Geir had to laugh. "It is what I hoped for, to be honest. But it's up to Beau to accept the post. I can't answer for him. I can only say that I'd welcome him as my partner in work as well as in mated life." Geir turned to Beau, seated on the other side of Jacki.

She would always be between them—in the best possible way. The three of them would share their lives and protect each other in every possible way. It was a beautiful vision of the future.

"I—" Beau started, his mouth opening and closing several times before he finally got the words out. "I'm amazed you would consider me for such a great responsibility on such short acquaintance," he finally said. "But I wholeheartedly accept. I've been looking for a purpose in my life for a long time. I knew Jacki was it when I first saw her, but I didn't really understand how full my life would become with her—and now all of you—in it. I feel like I'm home here, among the *pantera noir*, in a way I've never really felt before. And I will swear fealty to you, Ria and Jake, if you will have me, and work to the best of my ability for the betterment of the Clan for the rest of my days."

"Well spoken," Ria complimented Beau as she accepted his words. "Talk to Kinkaid tomorrow and straighten everything out. I want to install you all in your new roles as soon as possible. We need to start setting up house here in a big way. We may all be in one place, finally, and not forever running, but that doesn't mean we still don't have enemies out there, gunning for us." She looked pointedly at Harper. "It's clear we need to make preparations and set up routines now that we have a permanent home. I'd like to get started on that as quickly as we can."

Geir thought it was a sound strategy and said so. The rest of the meal passed in a happy daze for Geir as he contemplated all the amazing changes that had happened so unexpectedly. Life was good. Very good, indeed.

That night, after dinner and a strategy session where Geir and Beau mapped out the beginnings of a regular schedule for training and work, they went back to Jacki's room. Geir had been thinking about ways to improve the house for them as a trio, but he needed to know for certain that all of them were on the same page, once and for all.

Instead of following Jacki toward the bed and starting the seduction, as was their habit of the past few days, Geir signaled for Beau to hold back. Geir sat on the chair while

Beau sat quietly on the foot of the bed. Jacki realized they weren't crowding her and turned around.

"What's up?" she asked, an uncertain smile hovering around her lips.

"I want to build on to the house," Geir started speaking, uncertain how to approach the discussion of such serious matters.

"That sounds like a great idea," Jacki replied enthusiastically. "Can I help pick out the fixtures?"

"Of course you can," Geir said immediately. "We all need to have input on the design of our home. I just wanted to be certain it's what we all want. I know you both said you'd cut ties with the Kinkaid Clan and stay here with the *pantera noir*—with me. You have no idea how humbled I am that you're willing to relocate. I will do my utmost to make sure neither of you ever regret that decision."

"Don't sweat it, G-man," Beau replied casually, but Geir could see the seriousness in his eyes. "You and I have both bound our lives to Jacki. I figure wherever she is, is home." Beau held out a hand to Jacki and she took it, going over to sit next to him on the edge of the mattress. "Plus, I've been a rolling stone most of my life. I never had any strong ties to *tigre d'or*. I was a loner for a long time. I half expected to stay a loner 'til my dying day, which I fully expected to be on a battlefield somewhere. And then I saw Jacki and everything changed." Beau squeezed her hand and she rested her head against his shoulder, sitting at his side.

"I can't believe it took you so long even to talk to me. And you were so angry all the time," Jacki protested softly. "I thought you hated me."

"Never, sweetheart." Beau leaned down and kissed her hair before resuming his tale. "After I saw her that first time, I got my ass into Kinkaid's sphere of influence as fast as I could manage. Sam let me into the Clan, but though I was welcome there for my skills, I didn't have any real ties to them other than Jacki, and I could really only watch her from afar. She's like a princess to the Kinkaids. They put all the

Clan's selkies up on pedestals because they're so magical and so rare."

"It's not that bad," Jacki protested with a grin.

Beau made a face and nodded at Geir. "It *is* that bad. Trust me. I finally wangled my way onto yacht duty because I knew most of the selkies cycled through the ship's roster. And then she showed up with Tom, the most over-protective brother in the universe. He ran interference, for which I still owe him a beat-down once he's fully healed."

"Don't you dare!" Jacki objected, but she was grinning. They all knew Beau wouldn't beat up Tom. Not if he wanted to keep his mate happy—and keeping Jacki happy was the driving force of his existence now that they were mated.

"I have to think that if Tom hadn't been there, perhaps this threesome would never have formed. You two might have mated and Jacki and I might never have met," Geir observed, a sad weight on his heart when the thought registered in his mind.

Jacki got up and came over to him, sitting on his lap and putting her arms around his neck. Geir felt immediately better, though the doubt stuck with him. Was he really supposed to be in this relationship? Or was he the interloper?

"Don't ever think that, Geir." Jacki ran her hand through his hair, leaning her forehead against his. "I'm the High Priestess's apprentice. The Lady Herself had a hand in our mating and Bettina believes that all has happened according to the Goddess's plan for us. I'm not fey like Bettina. I have a lot of magic for a shifter, but I'm not up to her level. She's from another realm altogether, and if she falls, it's going to take everything I have—and all the support I can get from my mates as well—to even begin to fill her shoes. That's Bettina's theory and it feels right to me too. I was meant to be with both of you. That's why neither one of you alone were able to get close enough to mate me." She smiled and leaned in to press a sexy kiss on Geir's lips.

He considered her words with the tiny part of his brain that wasn't busy enjoying her kiss. What she said made sense, but he needed to be really sure before he surrendered the last of his doubts. When she broke off the kiss and looked deep into his eyes, he asked the most important question.

"Will you stay with me forever? Will the three of us be able to make this work for the rest of our lives?" Every one of his insecurities sounded in those words, but neither Jacki nor Beau seemed to think less of him for speaking his fears so plainly.

Beau stood and walked over to the chair, placing one hand on Geir's shoulder, and one on Jacki's back. His pose was very serious when he spoke.

"No one really knows every facet of their future. Not even people like Jake who get visions of what will be. What I can say is that I'm committed to loving and protecting Jacki for the rest of my days. Making her happy is now my first goal in life." Beau rubbed little circles on Jacki's back. "If that means partnering up with the most powerful *pantera noir* fighter of this age, well then, there are worse things I can think of doing with my life." Beau grinned. "Geir, you undervalue yourself all the time. You're a great man. One of the great protectors of this generation. I just got through telling you I've been an aimless, wandering, rolling stone most of my life. The fact that you're willing to put up with me, take me into your family, your adopted Clan, and give me a place to live and work where I can finally use all my talents to the best of their ability is like...it's like a miracle to me." Beau squeezed Geir's shoulder. "I think you're the one getting the raw end of this deal, buddy. You've opened up your home, your Clan, your workplace—every facet of your life to us. Are you sure *you* really want this? Because I have no doubt in my mind that I certainly do."

Geir breathed a huge sigh of relief. Now he just had to hear the words his heart craved from Jacki. Master Geir—Master sensei of the *pantera noir*—needed reassurance from his mate.

"I love you, Geir," she said softly, answering his unspoken need. "We'll make this work. One day at a time. There's nothing we can't do together and no obstacle we can't overcome." She smiled at him and the last cold finger of fear in his heart melted away for good. "I definitely want to help design the addition to the house. When can we start?"

"How about tomorrow? I've got some drawings I've been working on, but they're only preliminary. And they're in my office in the dojo," Geir added as Beau let go of his shoulder and moved away.

"Okay, but we'll need room to expand eventually. When the children come."

"Cubs?" Beau stilled, as did Geir. "You're not...?"

"Pregnant? No. Not yet," she said. "But with all the...um...activity we've been engaging in, don't you think it's sort of inevitable?"

Geir rested his head against her shoulder, stunned. "You have given me so much, Jacki," he whispered, emotion clogging his throat. "I've been alone a long time and I never thought to have a mate, cubs, and a brother too. I think I'm the one who hit the jackpot here." Geir raised his gaze to meet Beau's eyes and understanding flowed between them.

They had both gained so much by Jacki's presence in their lives. Yes, by the Goddess, this *would* work. They would make it work. Because the three of them together were stronger and better than any one of them was apart. Geir felt the rightness of that thought deep in his soul as he put the matter to rest once and for all.

Geir rose with Jacki still in his arms and carried her over to the giant bed. He placed her upon it, coming to rest at her side while Beau sat on the other side of the bed. Together, the men undressed her, stroking, licking and nibbling as they went, until she was naked and squirming with arousal before them.

This time he knew what he wanted and he was going to lead the others in a debauched dance of desire and passion. Jacki was in for a night of loving that he hoped she would never forget—for all the right reasons.

"So far, we've been running sprints, but I propose a

different approach tonight," Geir said almost conversationally as he ran his fingers across her breasts. Beau stilled and lifted his head from between her thighs.

"What sort of different approach?" Beau asked, a glint is his eye that Geir read as willingness to play along.

"Like I said, rather than a sprint...how about a marathon?" He felt Jacki's gasp of indrawn breath against his hand as he cupped her breast. "Do you like the sound of that, my little mate?"

She seemed unable to speak as Beau resumed going down on her, but she nodded, holding his gaze. Her pupils dilated with pleasure as Beau's actions pushed her to a small peak. He would see that look amplified over and over this night, if he had his way. All he had to do was sit back and try to keep the tiger in check.

Although...his inner cat seemed to be on board with this idea. He could feel it licking its chops in anticipation, but willing to wait, to give their mate the greatest possible pleasure. The cat was all about protecting, and pleasing, Jacki. It would do anything and everything for her—including dialing back its sexual aggression a bit, saving it for just the right time.

"Uh..." Jacki whispered even as her body shook with pleasure. Her breathing was ragged and would get more so if Geir had his way. He loved her curves. He could stroke her soft body for hours. "Were you thinking team event or relay?"

It took Geir a moment to understand her track and field reference. He grinned when he answered, loving the flush of pleasure on her face.

"Let's start with a relay and see where it leads," he replied and was gratified when she moaned in ecstasy as Beau brought her to another peak of pleasure.

Beau rose between her legs and took her, sliding deep into her body. He made the pleasure last, and Geir kept stroking her breasts, pinching and cupping, squeezing and teasing. She cried out when Beau moved deep within her. Geir watched avidly as her other mate brought her to greater and greater pleasure before finding his own.

Her body was still shaking when Beau moved away and Geir took his place. He rode her through the orgasm that was multiplying even as he began his own race to the finish. The cat rose to claim its mate in the most basic way possible, filling her with his essence. When she exploded in one last, brilliant fireball of passion, he was right there with her, shooting out to the stars and back again, in her arms.

When their breathing slowed, long moments later, it was Beau who lifted Jacki into his arms and walked with her into the attached bathroom. He had been busy while Geir was taking their mate, preparing a warm tub of water for her. Geir arrived in the doorway in time to see Beau lower Jacki into the water, her sighs of contentment filling the small room.

"The water up here is very pure," she mumbled with her eyes closed as steam wafted around her gorgeous body. "I bet it's taken from a mountain spring, rather than a well or some kind of treatment plant. This is pure. Fresh. Delicous."

She visibly held her breath as she dunked her head, sliding down into the deep, claw-footed tub and staying there for quite some time as the men watched.

Beau looked at Geir when she'd been under for a full minute at least. "She is a seal, right?"

Geir understood the slight panic. Neither of them would allow anything bad to happen to their mate.

"She looks okay. In fact, she's smiling," Geir pointed out. "Maybe she's testing us?"

"Teasing us, more like," Beau rumbled, clearly not happy with Jacki's chosen method of testing his patience.

"Do you want to be the one to drag her out of the water?" Geir asked. "I bet she has a plan for that. And I'm also betting whichever one of us does it, isn't going to like the results."

Beau growled in reply.

Jacki seemed to hear the growl and finally lifted herself out of the water, still smiling. "You guys are learning," she said, her tone complimentary.

Beau growled again. Geir, surprisingly, felt mellow. He would gladly learn whatever it was Jacki wanted to teach him. It had been a long time since he'd been a student, but he would do anything for his mate, including allowing her to reverse their roles any time she wanted.

Beau was not a happy man. He knew he was taking things too seriously, but even the tiniest hint of perceived danger to Jacki set him off. He hadn't liked the worry she just gave him. In his head, he knew she was a seal and she could do things in water that he could only dream of, but his head wasn't in charge when he saw her in that water, not breathing. Possibly in trouble and finding his worry funny. It hurt him, deep down inside. He couldn't deal with it, and the anger rose.

"I can't be here right now," he growled, turning to leave the room.

Geir's arm blocked his path out the bathroom door. He heard water sluice down Jacki's curvy body as she got up and stepped out of the tub.

"I'm sorry, Beau." Her soft voice was accompanied by her touch on his back. She walked right up to him, forming her body around him from behind, hugging his tense shoulders. "I didn't mean to tease you. I was okay, really. I would never put myself in danger. Not on purpose."

Beau turned around, unable to deny the plea in her voice. His upset had upset her as well and he regretted it. He didn't want to hear that note of distress in her voice—ever. He hugged her close, rocking her for a moment as he tried to get his emotions to settle down.

"Don't ever tease me about your safety," he said softly, near her ear. "I can't take it. My tiger goes nuts and it stirs up all kinds of bad memories."

She drew slightly away, cupping his cheek in one hand and looking deep into his eyes. Her gaze was filled with loving concern.

"Memories?" she asked. He supposed she had a right to

know, even if it was still hard for him to talk about.

"I think I told you that my mother was a priestess. She ministered to a small wolf Pack down on the bayou when my dad stumbled across her path. They were happy for many years. I was seventeen when they died. They were attacked by a local witch doctor who had made it his job to chase all shifters out of the parish. My mother stood in his way and he decided to make an example of her. He came after her with his people and there were too many. My father died protecting her, but he wasn't enough. They both died that night and then the next day, I killed my first mage. The witch doctor fell to my claws, but it could never bring back my mother. My father. Our happy home." He knew his voice was harsh with unshed misery, but he needed to get the story out. She needed to know the damage inside him if she was going to stay his mate. "My father couldn't protect my mother, but I will do everything in my power to protect my mate. I'm sorry, Jacki. It's an old wound."

Jacki soothed him throughout his tale of horror and pain, stroking his shoulders and resting her head in the crook of his neck. She kissed his collar bone and chin, murmuring reassurances that she would never tease him like that again. She apologized over and over, but he shushed her. She had nothing to be sorry for. He was the one who just couldn't deal with certain kinds of teasing. He would work on it, he promised her, but it would take a while to undo the trauma of the past.

She vowed to be there for him through it all. And then she kissed him.

At some point, Geir steered her toward the big shower at the other end of the room and she went, still kissing Beau. He backed her up against the wall even as the water started to flow and steam filled the air. Geir was taking care of them. She would have to thank him for his thoughtfulness later, but for now, she needed to soothe Beau. Her surprisingly sensitive mate who had deeper scars on his soul than she had realized.

She lifted her legs to wrap around his hips as he thrust into her and then there was nothing but movement and sound. Pleasure and promises. Joy and reassurance.

Beau loved her hard and fast, against the shower wall as the water shushed over them, enhancing the experience for her. When it was over, Geir was there to support her under the water as Beau took a seat on the small tile ledge at one end of the big shower stall.

She felt almost boneless, but Geir held her up, soaping her body and caring for her in the intimate ways of a mate. His every touch spoke of his care for her and before long, she felt her desire rise once more. When he positioned her with her face toward the wall of the shower, she wasn't sure what he had in mind, but then he bent his knees and entered her from behind, the water slick between their bodies.

He pumped hard and fast and within moments he was growling in her ear as she screamed his name, the sound echoing off the tile to bounce around the room. They stood together under the spray for a long moment after, letting the water take away any aches and pains, all thoughts of tomorrow or yesterday. There was only now. And now was damn fine, indeed.

EPILOGUE

The next morning, Harper Sagtakos sat with Ben Steel and the High Priestess Bettina at the dining room table long after the others had left to start their day. Geir, Beau and Jacki were down at the dojo. Tad and Mandy had moved back to their place with their cub. Harper wasn't sure where the Nyx and her mate were, but he assumed they would be showing up soon to get his answer on their proposition.

Harper had spent a good portion of the night in meditation and prayer. He had sought the guidance of the Great Spirit and he thought he knew what he was supposed to do. He had made a decision and it felt right in his heart. Now he just had to speak his truth to the others and watch how they would react.

Ben had spent the last twenty minutes going over strategies for ways he could support Harper as a double agent, if he agreed to the scheme. Bettina had simply sat and watched, her ageless gaze giving away little of her thoughts. Harper was at peace with his decision. He sat quietly and let the day unfold around him. His spirit was calm, which told him he had made the right decision.

Ria and Jake arrived with their ever-present security and sat down at the table. There was a calmness about the couple that appealed greatly to Harper. He had already learned much from these shapeshifters and their allies. He hoped the relationship would continue long into the future—and it would, if Jake's prophecy should truly come to pass. Harper looked forward to finding out if Jake really was as good a seer as everyone claimed.

After greetings of the day were exchanged, Ria and Jake faced Harper across the span of the wooden table. They watched him carefully as if gauging his every move, but he had trained himself to motionlessness. He was at peace.

"So what's the verdict?" Ria asked. "Will you help us protect ourselves, and perhaps clean up the evil infiltration into the *Altor Custodis*, by being our man inside?"

Everyone seemed to hold their breath in anticipation of his answer, but really, there was only one possible response. His meditations had told him that not only his entire future, but that of many innocent and good people, depended on his decision. It was a weighty responsibility, but Harper wasn't weak. He had trained most of his life for this. There was only one real choice…

"I'm in."

# # #

ABOUT THE AUTHOR

Bianca D'Arc has run a laboratory, climbed the corporate ladder in the shark-infested streets of lower Manhattan, studied and taught martial arts, and earned the right to put a whole bunch of letters after her name, but she's always enjoyed writing more than any of her other pursuits. She grew up and still lives on Long Island, where she keeps busy with an extensive garden, several aquariums full of very demanding fish, and writing her favorite genres of paranormal, fantasy and sci-fi romance.

Bianca loves to hear from readers and can be reached through Twitter (@BiancaDArc), Facebook (BiancaDArcAuthor) or through the various links on her website.

WELCOME TO THE D'ARC SIDE...
WWW.BIANCADARC.COM

OTHER BOOKS BY BIANCA D'ARC

Now Available

Brotherhood of Blood
One & Only
Rare Vintage
Phantom Desires
Sweeter Than Wine
Forever Valentine
Wolf Hills
Wolf Quest

Tales of the Were
Lords of the Were
Inferno

Tales of the Were – The Others
Rocky
Slade

Tales of the Were – Redstone Clan
Grif
Red
Magnus
Bobcat
Matt

String of Fate
Cat's Cradle
King's Throne
Jacob's Ladder
Her Warriors

Guardians of the Dark
Half Past Dead
Once Bitten, Twice Dead
A Darker Shade of Dead
The Beast Within
Dead Alert

Dragon Knights
Maiden Flight
The Dragon Healer
Border Lair
Master at Arms
The Ice Dragon
Prince of Spies
Wings of Change
FireDrake
Dragon Storm
Keeper of the Flame

Resonance Mates
Hara's Legacy
Davin's Quest
Jaci's Experiment
Grady's Awakening
Harry's Sacrifice

Jit'Suku Chronicles
Arcana: King of Swords
Arcana: King of Cups
Arcana: King of Clubs
End of the Line

StarLords: Hidden Talent

Gifts of the Ancients
Warrior's Heart

Print Anthologies
Ladies of the Lair
I Dream of Dragons Vol. 1
Brotherhood of Blood
Caught by Cupid

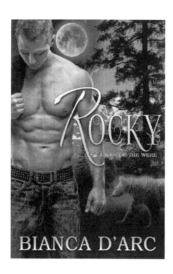

TALES OF THE WERE ~ THE OTHERS
ROCKY

On the run from her husband's killers, there is only one man who can help her now… her Rock.

Maggie is on the run from those who killed her husband nine months ago. She knows the only one who can help her is Rocco, a grizzly shifter she knew in her youth. She arrives on his doorstep in labor with twins. Magical, shapeshifting, bear cub twins destined to lead the next generation of werecreatures in North America.

Rocky is devastated by the news of his Clan brother's death, but he cannot deny the attraction that has never waned for the small human woman who stole his heart a long time ago. Rocky absented himself from her life when she chose to marry his childhood friend, but the years haven't changed the way he feels for her.

And now there are two young lives to protect. Rocky will do everything in his power to end the threat to the small family and claim them for himself. He knows he is the perfect Alpha to teach the cubs as they grow into their power… if their mother will let him love her as he has always longed to do.

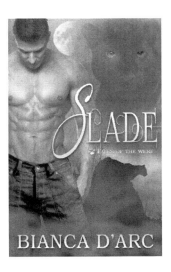

TALES OF THE WERE ~ THE OTHERS
SLADE

The fate of all shifters rests on his broad shoulders, but all he can think of is her.

Slade is a warrior and spy sent to Nevada to track a brutal murderer before the existence of all shifters is revealed to a world not ready to know.

Kate is a priestess serving the large community of shifters that have gathered around the Redstone cougars. When their matriarch is murdered and the scene polluted by dark magic, she knows she must help the enigmatic man sent to track the killer.

Together, Slade and Kate find not one but two evil mages that they alone can neutralize. Slade finds it hard to keep his hands off his sexy new partner, the cougars are out for blood, and the killers have an even more sinister plan in mind.

Can Kate somehow keep her hands to herself when the most attractive man she's ever met makes her want to throw caution to the wind? And can Slade do his job and save the situation when he's finally found a woman who can make him purr?

Warning: Contains a tiny bit of sexy ménage action with two smokin' hot men..

TALES OF THE WERE ~ REDSTONE CLAN 1
GRIF

Griffon Redstone is the eldest of five brothers and the leader of one of the most influential shifter Clans in North America. He seeks solace in the mountains, away from the horrific events of the past months, for both himself and his young sister. The deaths of their older sister and mother have hit them both very hard.

Lindsey Tate is human, but very aware of the werewolf Pack that lives near her grandfather's old cabin. She's come to right a wrong her grandfather committed against the Pack and salvage what's left of her family's honor—if the wolves will let her. Mostly, they seem intent on running her out of town on a rail.

But the golden haired stranger, Grif, comes to her rescue more than once. He stands up for her against the wolf Pack and then helps her fix the old generator at the cabin. When she performs a ceremony she expects will end in her death, the shifter deity has other ideas. Thrown together by fate, neither of them can deny their deep attraction, but will an old enemy tear them apart?

Warning: Frisky cats get up to all sorts of naughtiness, including a frenzy-induced multi-partner situation that might be a little intense for some readers.

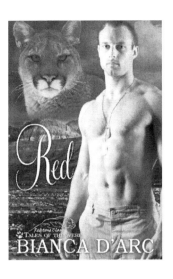

TALES OF THE WERE ~ REDSTONE CLAN 2
RED

A water nymph and a werecougar meet in a bar fight… No joke.

Steve Redstone agrees to keep an eye on his friend's little sister while she's partying in Las Vegas. He's happy to do the favor for an old Army buddy. What he doesn't expect is the wild woman who heats his blood and attracts too much attention from Others in the area.

Steve ends up defending her honor, breaking his cover and seducing the woman all within hours of meeting her, but he's helpless to resist her. She is his mate and that startling fact is going to open up a whole can of worms with her, her brother and the rest of the Redstone Clan.

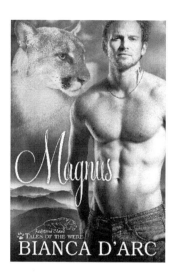

TALES OF THE WERE ~ REDSTONE CLAN 3
MAGNUS

A tortured vampire, a lonely shifter, and a deadly power struggle of supernatural proportions. Can their forbidden love prevail?

Magnus is the quiet brother. The one who keeps to himself. But he has good reason for his loner status. Two years ago, he met a woman. Not just any woman. This woman made his inner cougar stand up and roar. Even in human form, he purred when she stroked him, a sure sign that she was his mate. And mating is a very serious thing among shifters. Too bad the lady had fangs...

Mag discovers Miranda being held captive. She's been tortured to the point of -madness. Mag frees her and takes her to his home, nursing her back to health and defying all convention to keep her with him. He doesn't ever want to let her go again, but he knows the deck is stacked against them.

When a vampire uprising threatens, Mag and Miranda are in the middle. More than just their necks are on the line when a group of vampires seek to kill them and overthrow the current Master. But they have powerful allies, and their renewed relationship has made both of them stronger than either would ever be alone.

Can they stay together forever? Or will the daylight—and their two very different worlds—tear them apart again?

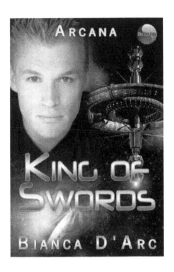

ARCANA
KING OF SWORDS

David is a newly retired special ops soldier, looking to find his way in an unfamiliar civilian world. His first step is to visit an old friend, the owner of a bar called *The Rabbit Hole* on a distant space station. While there, he meets an intriguing woman who holds the keys to his future.

Adele has a special ability, handed down through her family. Adele can sometimes see the future. She doesn't know exactly why she's been drawn to the space station where her aunt deals cards in a bar that caters to station workers and ex-military. She only knows that she needs to be there. When she meets David, sparks of desire fly between them and she begins to suspect that he is part of the reason she traveled halfway across the galaxy.

Pirates gas the inhabitants of the station while Adele and David are safe inside a transport tube and it's up to them to repel the invaders. Passion flares while they wait for the right moment to overcome the alien threat and retake the station. But what good can one retired soldier and a civilian do against a ship full of alien pirates?

WWW.BIANCADARC.COM

Made in the USA
San Bernardino, CA
27 November 2014